Patina

#1

—

P.S. Clinen

Patina #1

First Published In 2024 By

P.S. Clinen

No part of this document may be reproduced without written consent from the author.

All Rights Reserved

Copyright © 2024 P.S. Clinen

ISBN-13: 979-8-327-16431-4

More from the author can be found at psclinen.com

Also by P.S. Clinen:

Tenebrae Manor

A Boy Named Art

The Will of the Wisp

Vignettes – An Anthology

Trick Shots – The Lyrics of Pinnacle Tricks

Contents

Knock Terns 19

Prologue – Astral Trees 26

Fairy Chimneys 30

The Convent 38

Panjandrum 47

The Incumbent & the Challenger 57

On the Train to Banksia 72

The Woodnote Boys 84

Captain Ivy Festoon 96

Of Frost-Bitten Fields 111

Mortal Curse 120

A Strange Thing Happens 140

Gull & Leviathan – A Fable 148

Holes in the History of Things 152

Mawson's Journal 160

Impossible Patience 177

Clairvoyance 186

The Disclaimer 198

Polly & Silas 209

The Fourth Reflection 223

"Are You There?" 234

Tower of Fog	252
The Shaman	260
Brooding Over Brews	277
Sticks & Stones	287
Creaking of the Beam	300
Afterforward	316

For someone.

"'God save thee, ancient Mariner!

From the fiends, that plague thee thus! —

Why look'st thou so?' — With my cross-bow

I shot the ALBATROSS."

- Samuel Taylor Coleridge

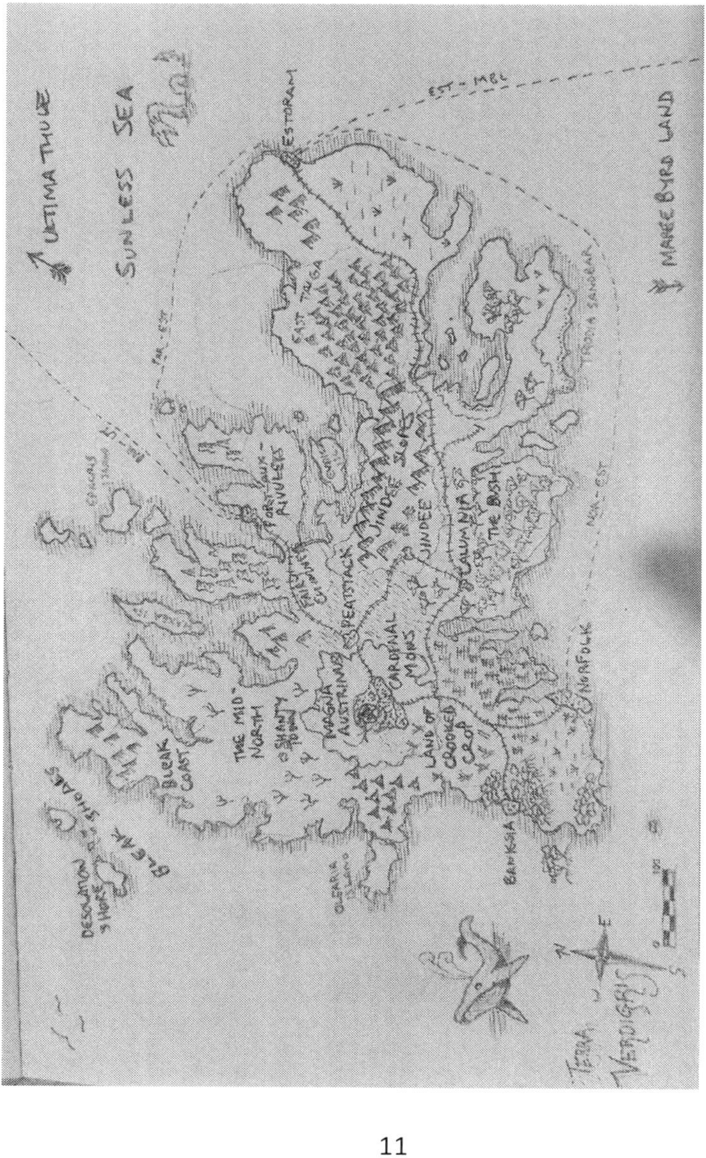
ULTIMA THULE
SUNLESS SEA
ESTORAN
EST - MBL
MAKEE BYRD LAND
DESOLATION SHORE
BLEAK COAST
THE MID-NORTH
SPEATSTACK
CARDINAL MONS
LAND OF CROOKED CROP
JINDEE
THE BUSH
NORFOLK
BANKSIA
TERRA
VERDIGRIS

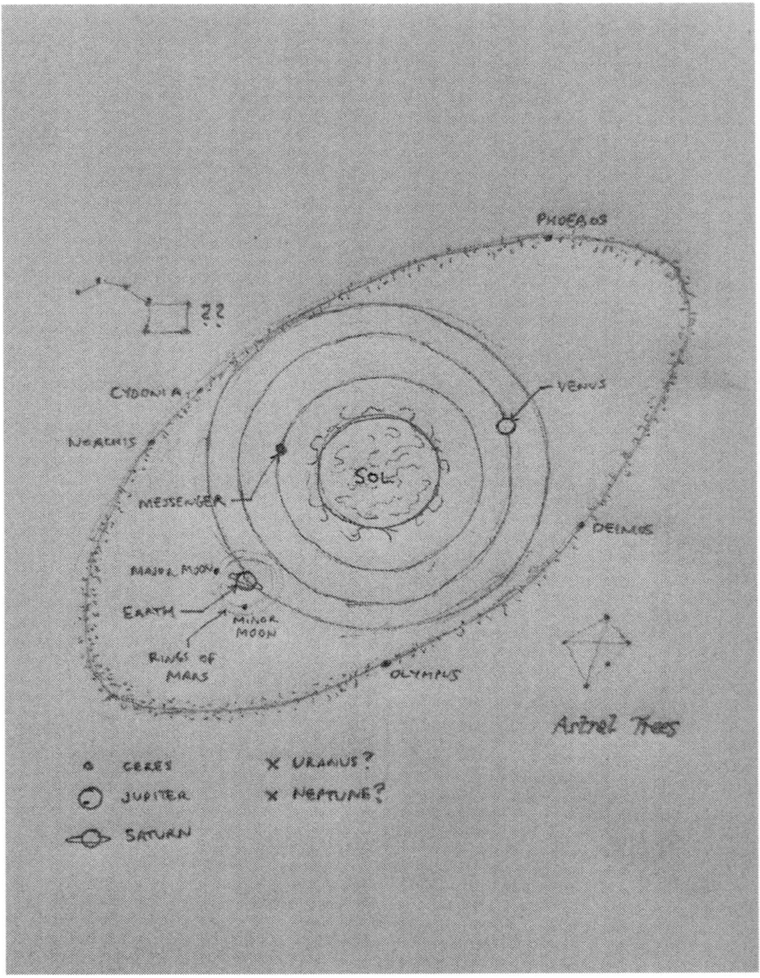

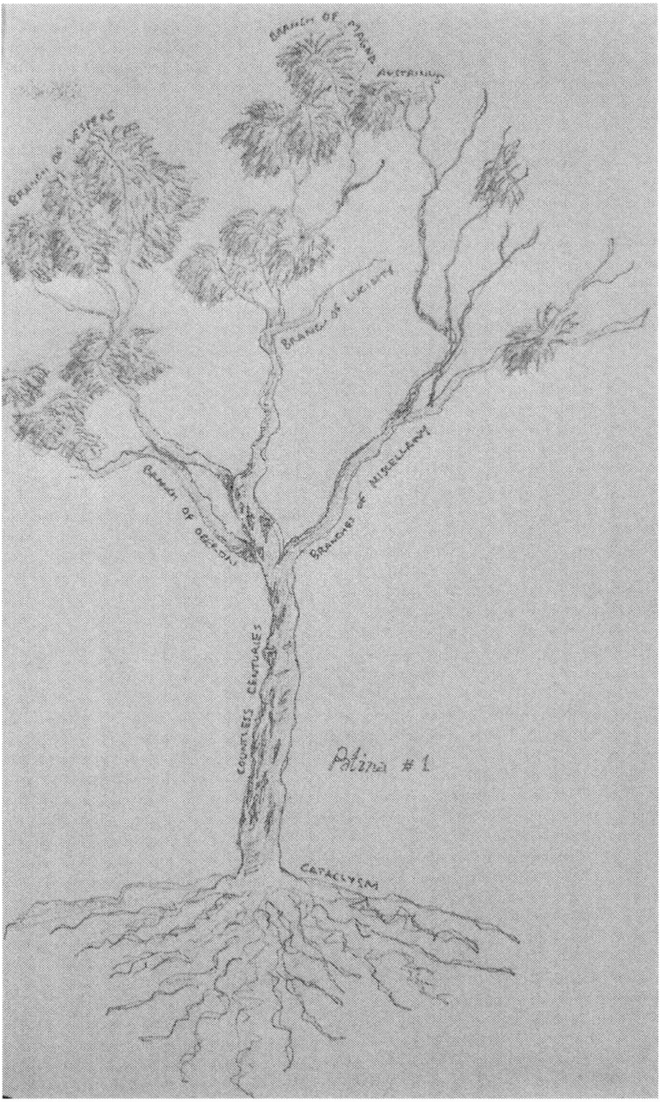
COUNTLESS CENTURIES
CATACLYSM
Patina #1

Cast of characters (in order of appearance)

LUCIDA GREEN – a young adventurer
BYRNE – a peddler
CAPTAIN OF THE S.S. HOBART
LIBRA TENEBRIFIC – leader of Verdigris
NAMELESS WOMAN – Byrne's customer
MAREE BIRD *(mentioned)* – Hobart captain's ex-wife

DELANEY VESPERS – student of Calumnia Convent
MADAM NUNWISER – teacher at Calumnia Convent
FRANCIS – a student

PAN / JAN / DRUM – bumbling city officials, brothers
POLLY JEAN CUPIO – Libra's assistant
AUSTIN SPINDLE – opposition leader of Verdigris
SILAS KRUMMHOLZ – Spindle's assistant

VITUS – man on the train
YOWIE GALIMATIAS – man on the train
TRAIN GUARDS

RHENEAS WOODNOTE – a young boy
BALFOUR WOODNOTE – his brother
PIDGIE – friend of the Woodnote boys

CAPTAIN IVY FESTOON – ship captain

SQUABBLE / VALENTINE / BRINE – her crew

IGGY OBERON – local loser of Mid-North shanty town

THORN-PETAL – resident of Mid-North shanty town

COLDCHOP – shaman of Mid-North shanty town

MUTT & CHURL – children of Mid-North shanty town

FOLDCLOP *(mentioned)* – Coldchop's brother

ROSIE – resident of Mid-North shanty town

NAMELESS MAN – protagonist of Mortal Curse

ASHEN – his friend

ELLAMENO PEA – a charlatan

ASHEN'S COUSIN

NAMELESS MAN'S MOTHER

STYMPHALES – resident hunter of Mid-North shanty town

ARTEMIS – resident hunter of Mid-North shanty town

ODINA – student of Calumnia Convent

MAWSON – second mate of Ultima Thule expedition

CAPTAIN BYRD – captain of Ultima Thule expedition

BELLINGHAM *(deceased)* / BROTHER OF BELLINGHAM / FALCONER *(deceased)* / AMUND

/ DAVIS / CASEY / MR. SOLANDER / FINCH / McMURDO / UNAMED SHIP HAND – crew of Ultima Thule expedition

WALLACE WOODNOTE – father of Rheneas & Balfour
HIS UNNAMED WIFE – mother of Rheneas & Balfour
FIGLEY *(deceased) (mentioned)*

THE ADJUDICATOR
THE STENOGRAPHER
POLLY JEAN'S UNNAMED PARENTS

LEWISTON – an amateur writer
THE THING IN THE ELEVATOR - ???

DAVYD TRIPTYCH – an over-worked truck driver
HIS BOSS
THE OWNER OF BLEAK BREAK POINT
CARDIGAN JONES – a mysterious man

GREYWAITE – a hermit
FLAGCLOAK – his one visitor

THE SHAMAN – an outcast
WILLIE WAGTAIL – his fellow outcast

ORION – your average everyman
SABINA – his wife

THEIR CHILD
SUZAN – barkeep
RODNEY – local drunk
RYAN *(mentioned)* – barkeep

TREEN – niece of Vitus
McKENNARK *(mentioned)* – elderly resident of Banksia
ELANOR – Treen's mother
MOTHER OF ELANOR & VITUS – a senile woman
DOUG – Treen's brother
KITTY – Treen's sister
LUKEY – Banksian store owner *(mentioned)*

ERNIE BURSTWHILE – a police officer
HIS WIFE *(deceased) (mentioned)*
TABBY GARTH – a police officer
DADDY LONG-LEGS – a mysterious man
HALROY – Peatstack factory owner *(mentioned)*
ASTRID – Ernie's daughter
TRISH – her daughter
MANNY *(mentioned)* – Ernie's son

Knock Terns

Knock-knock.

The percussive thrum sounded itself through the bush. First here, now there, followed by nowhere at all. Then it came again – *knock knock* – louder this time, cutting through the hazy warmth of the spring morning. The cicadas added their own tremolo symphony; a din where any renegade sound would be lost in the sonic fuzz. Not a noise, it would seem, could crest that static dirge, until then the percussion sounded again – *knock-knock*.

When it appeared that nobody observed the foetid creek, heard the savage isolation of the insects, or smelled the cloying medicinal scent of the eucalypt (and indeed it would seem nobody did any of these things), the girl charged forward from the shade of the juniper and piqued those artful senses. She broke the tranquil chaos, stood lithe as a panther, and eyed the grass in her hand with a magpie fascination.

Knock-knock.

There it was again. It called to her through the rustling of gum leaves, carried its beat betwixt the gnarled agony of Joshua tree branches. The girl dragged a strand of dark hair off her face, coated in sweat, and clasped her teeth down onto her blade of grass. A tooth pick, no - a cigarette (for all the coolest folk smoked) – she would pretend it was a smoke. She breathed deeply of her faux cigarette and found her lungs filled instead with the pollen of wattle; her freckled face contorted, plasticised, and she let loose an almighty and un-lady-like sneeze that shook her body and sent the finches scattering air bound. Her wine-coloured eyes scanned the surroundings – ha ha! Nobody had seen the undignified act.

Whoosh.

No knocking this time. Just the beat of a different kind; the fluttered *whomp-whomp* of wings, that of a bird perching on her shoulder. The avian denizen promptly prodded its beak upon the girl's collar. No *knock-knock,* more of a *tap-tap* on the faded leather of her tunic.

"Late again," she smirked.

The bird spread its maroon crest in retort, before forgetting it was ever insulted and turned to preening its midnight wings. A Knock Tern – and this one belonged to Lucida Green – an intelligent bird that conveyed messages through some secret language of pecky-pecking on tree trunks.

"You've scratched yourself again, bird," said Lucida, "Silly Nettles."

But Nettles didn't care; knock terns spent their fledgling days hidden in brambles, the thorns warding off predators at the expense of a scritch-a-scratch to their young feathers. He took the strip of grass from Lucida's hand and, realising that it wasn't food, cast it aside with a confident toss of the head.

"Anything?" she asked.

"Caw!" cried Nettles, and he took flight and perched on the branch of a nearby eucalypt.

Knock knock – no.

"I don't believe you,"

Nettles preened his breast, sending feathers drifting downward, while the bird procured a dull brass object as if from nowhere. The rusted thing still glinted slightly in the morning light.

"Ha! I knew it!" Lucida cried, "Cough it up, bird-brain."

With a confidence that one only ever saw in a child such as her, Lucida thrust forth her palm expectantly, her other palm shoved against her hip – like a little teapot short and stout. As Nettles fluttered down to her she recalled that rhyme her nanny had often sung to her, the words whistling through her head in a whirlwind of feathers and memories. And when the dust had settled, and Nettles had reluctantly given up the only possession he had, Lucida gazed down at the corroded cog that sat in her palm like a dusk-washed rose. It was a tiny thing, but no doubt it had once been a vital piece in some ancient machine. She pondered its unassuming façade, personified the corroded scrap and imagined it as underappreciated by other larger cogs. And now the years had sunk their wolf fangs into its sheen, left it to forget its function and disintegrate into the dusk of time.

"Needs a polish," she muttered, and all of a sudden the cog was her favourite thing in the world.

It was a lucky trinket – it had to be; it had found her; she had found it. She would take care of the neglected little thing. Lucida clasped the cog to her chest, squeezing it with such force that it might have crumbled were it more rusted than it was. Dropping to one knee, Lucida procured her dagger from her belt and cut herself a strip of reed growing miserably by the creek bed. No point in rinsing it – the tarn was still, and anything dipped beneath into its shallows would probably come out dirtier than when it was submerged. She braided two reeds together – like her own black pigtails – and looped the little cog onto her new makeshift necklace. *Perfect.* Pleased with her handiwork she rose and sighed; Nettles grumbled from his perch.

"Are you still here, Nettles?"

Nettles had turned his head a full hemisphere, so that his crest looked like a prominent beard. If he understood anything Lucida said to him, he certainly didn't seem to care. The two of them had lurked in The Bush for weeks now, and despite the occasional reference to civilisation (shown, for example, in the brass cog) they had not encountered another human being. Lucida arched her head back and squinted her eyes at the sunlight. Even behind the thin cloud cover the sun shone sharply; when Lucida blinked, she could still see the red stamp of it imprinted behind her eyelids. The breeze blew from whence she'd come, bringing with it the hope of a purpose, whispering through the gum leaves and exposing their white-green undersides. The finches cried softly but sternly – even they knew their role, and as Lucida spied a lazy lizard languishing on a warm rock, she realised all at once that she was so alone. The heroes had already scoured this land; there was nothing left to discover. She was too late to work the mines that sat abandoned in The Bush; they too had been scavenged for all their worth by the men who, taking their profits, had marched back to The City with a swag of fortune, leaving nothing behind but the by-products of their labour. A cart here, a steel rail warped by heat and moisture – time had left Lucida behind, even though the discovery she longed to experience lay rooted in the past.

"Nettles," she repeated, less sure, "are you still here?"

During her daydream the bird had taken to scratching at the ground with his talons, and once hearing the uncertain sadness in his master's voice he raced to her shoulder and nuzzled her with an animal absence. He might not have understood her 'people' emotions, but there was enough in common betwixt the two creatures for him to comprehend her need for company at that moment. Lucida managed a smile and thought of family, of friendships; there weren't many left, but at least she had her Knock Tern, her wandering feet, her unending thirst for adventure.

"The Steppe must be close," said Lucida, "might see things a bit clearer from there."

Nettles tapped once on her shoulder, *yes*.

"Spring follows Winter, remember what nanny said?"

Knock – yes.

With that the bird took off, his crest a bloodstained streak through the canopy, then gone, but not for long. Lucida knew he'd return once he had found something; for Spring indeed followed Winter, and Lucida's longing for a deserved Summer could, for all she knew, have been closer than ever.

Prologue – Astral Trees

It so happened every August, when the year was at its coldest, that the sky above outfit itself with celestial accoutrements so resplendent that the population of Verdigris could only marvel in awe. The light of stars from bygone epochs had finally arrived, and could not but feel, after travelling so far, cheated to appear as just one mote of light on the umbrageous canvas. But to downplay their pulchritude was a disservice to their long journey, and each ornament shone with a deserved grandeur both gracious in its mystery and dignified in its silence. It was beauty unparalleled by any handful of greenstone or malachite, or any lunar blossom of wattle or grevillea; artists would attempt to capture it in their washes, the poets would write of it in their nocturnes, and scholars would piece together the little dots into schematics, as though the night were presenting instructions to its inner workings for them to decode. The spires of the great capital city of Magna Austrinus ascended in the way made clear by stars, and reached in vain from the peak of Cardinal Mons for that which could not be held in hands.

For this month alone, the Moon would gaze down on Earth with accompaniment; the Minor Moon would rise into view from the vermillion dusk to spin a web for itself next to its full-bellied parent. Hereon Major and Minor would embrace in silence with the affection of friends reunited after a long journey, and light up the evenings with a brilliant luminance made possible by the rays refracted off the Rings of Mars. For the people of Verdigris, it was an annual celebration of the cosmos, as well as an admonition to understand a knowledge that had been lost to them; for there were none left alive who knew of that age of darkness - when the night was lit by one lantern - or of the calamitous event that led to its downfall. There were things known and things extirpated, eaten away like a page in a dusty book, and even the most learned of Verdigris' citizens saw their world in the light of an incomplete jigsaw puzzle rather than breaking any new trodden ground. Yes, there were discoveries made all the time, but it was known that knowledge had been gathered up by a previous generation, one that had met an end that scattered all its thoughts and ideals like a dropped bag of marbles - those of this new age were simply tidying up the mess.

An obvious precedent was the phenomenon known as the Rings of Mars. That curved brush stroke glittering across the sky for one season of the year - the way it rose and set and curled and swept - could only discern that the Earth was a globe, and while the people of Verdigris were utterly adamant that this was true, no woman or man had ever travelled the circumference to confirm it. True, an age of steam had accelerated the methods with which the pioneers could explore, but new challenges always appeared - wild seas, vicious winds, or a 'Land Ho!' met with barren shorelines that were completely uninhabitable. Verdigris was the only sustainable landmass known, and as such, Earth's perimeter was uncharted, its dimensions concealed, and the brilliant reds of Mars' Rings spun silently in the sky, revealing what it could, in the only language it knew how to speak.

And from below those reds - the crimson, the rose, the coral and cardinal - splashed against the brilliant navy blue of night, on the *terra firma* of the southerly land of Verdigris, the great minds pondered desperately on those times long past. The maps that remained were enough to spark a childlike fascination - where massive lands were sketched with cities and settlements dotted across them like grains of sand on the beach - a question of how so much of the world had been colonised and obviously liveable. Why was it that Verdigris was the only land awash with life? Why did the trees thrive here and not there, or the waters expunge themselves of poison inland, but the great sea beyond was salted beyond measure? The blooms of the trees yearned to know its roots, to understand that which nourished them, and humanity made its way down the branches of time - some like scurrying beetles, others like dead leaves falling towards a revelation they could no longer share, and the bark of the trunks carved with omnipotent mystery cloaked the enigma of existence, be it divine creation or indifferent accident. The moons knew, the rings knew, the light of stars from times gone - they knew.

Fairy Chimneys

Beneath the backdrop of the fairy chimneys, beyond which stretched the moon-scaped Steppe of Selene, the harbour town of Port-Aux-Rivulets was brimming with a flurry of excitement. For their annual celebration of the Major-Minor Festival was well underway, and the marshy rivers that fed the sea from inland had begun to thaw and herald a new season forthcoming. The citizens could stroll the cobbled streets and throw their heads back in jubilee, as the buntings of coloured flags were kissed by the breeze of spring's harbinger, and observe - misty-eyed - the rose gold beauty of cliff formations in the dusky light of the setting sun. The serpentine ribbons of glassy water that slipped slowly from the canyons sidled beneath the Selene Bridge connecting the larger southern part of town with the smaller north. Here on the bridge a busking of musicians filled the air with the wheeze of accordions and the thrum of the cello, and the painters resolutely ignored the smell of the fish crates while they tried to capture the harbour scene on canvas. For many it was the best time of the year. Yet there would soon be another call for celebration when the Steamship Hobart pulled into port, its long-awaited return bringing with it a discovery of monumental status: news of another land discovered. And so, in spite of the setting sun splitting its rays betwixt the jagged jutting of hoodoo formations signalling the end of another day, the townsfolk basked in a dawn light of newly hatched possibility. The jubilee would no doubt continue throughout the evening, and for those who manned the many market stalls along the quay, the busy day was about to carry on a little longer. Sporting a grand view of the great ship was one such merchant named Byrne, who preferred to gaze wistfully at the Steamship Hobart rather than match the feverish scurrying of his contemporaries, who frantically restocked their wares for the approaching evening. While fruit crates were unloaded and trinkets were polished, Byrne sat stationary on his nest of stock with a calm that suited a man approaching the end of his middle age. His treasures would sell - they always did, and it was not as though he was struggling to make a living, now that his wife was gone, and children had grown up and flown. No, he saw the importance of what was happening - this ship had returned with an important discovery; this was one of those 'once-in-a-lifetime' events. He would regret wasting these hours performing the perfunctory acts of any other random day.

Byrne had run this stand for two decades, and his treasures were of a bygone era, knickknacks of esoteric origin that even he himself could not know. He was but a messenger, as he would oft say; a merchant who had merely come upon an item and wished only to impart it to an appropriate owner - *for a small fee of course*. The old books he had gathered, many of which he had not read himself, propped themselves against one another like elderly gentlemen steadied by weary nurses, with titles that inspired the fantastic - 'Master and Margarita', 'Titus Groan', 'Nightwood' and 'Orlando'. Books about killing mockingbirds or flying over cuckoo's nests, even some that were written in another language, like the strange block-like letters that stood boldly above the understood title of 'Dead Souls'. Some spines were stiff and threatened to crumble upon the slightest touch, others as limp and fragile as moth wings, where the mere grease of the average finger would stain it permanently.

"But who were these writers? And what of these mysterious languages?" A customer might say.

But for Byrne, that was all part of his showmanship, "Nobody knows! Such is the rarity of that piece you hold, be careful now! There may be no other copy!"

"Check this out," called one pigeon to another, "check this bottle… it's nice."

"Nice?" Byrne gasped in mock aghast, "that bottle is a prize! It implores us to *'enjoy Coca-Cola'*. Now you tell me, how does one do that?!"

Others couldn't let go of the strange languages written in the books, "Gibberish. Everyone knows we speak Strahlian."

Some people are just hard to please.

By now the crowd were growing restless with the anticipation of something, anything, to satiate the vibrancy of the carnival, and give meaning to the pomp and ceremony. A dais had been erected near the water's edge, from which barrels and luggage were trafficked off the ship, along with the odd sailor here or there.

Would someone of status appear tonight? To welcome these folk on their return home? Damn politicians don't care anyway...

But then, Byrne realised that the evening was coming to a head. Through the avian scuttle of the crowd, he saw *her*. Plump as possible, with a dignity matching her girth, she waded through; the onlookers peeled away from her, moons pushed from their mother orbit, driftwood sent tumbling on lunar tides - *make way, make way*. How was it that she could move such weight so gracefully? She mounted the dais, gravity ignored, and turned to drink in the cheers of the crowd. Byrne observed the eruption of dark hair from atop her head, the lacquered quivering of paunch, the pallid curve of upper arms - everything about her threatened to burst, yet not of some volcanic explosion, rather a pressured pop of one grown drum tight, dense as a dying star, from inward to out. Yet there she remained standing, all contained in such expanse, and in complete owning of her people before her.

Her voice was strong, though perhaps of a higher pitch than one might have thought, and she waxed lyrical of the crew who had returned, and returned with a discovery of an icy land far to the south that had long been suspected but never observed. There was a panache in the woman's words - perhaps a roll of the eyes, as though *she* could have made such a discovery herself, and *easily*, if only she'd chosen to. She gave due complements at the magnitude of such a discovery - new lands where the population might spread - and looked down her nose at just the right angle as if to remind the people that she was their leader. Democratic though her leadership might have been, to her it was a monarchy, such was the vanity of Miss Libra Tenebrific.

The crowd were elated, the Rings of Mars sparkled in the sunset sky, and Byrne was feeling suddenly lacking; a husk, drained of all energy or appeal. An insect succumbing to her spider poison, though such a death was welcomed. He had never known of romantic love, though he'd married and had children, his wife had never been one to show much emotion; as such he'd never experienced the concept of being so valuable to another person, and seeing the leader of Verdigris in all her nocturnal beauty, lavished in praise by a crowd that might have assumed that it was *her* who had returned from the grand adventure, a childish longing cried out from within him. He saw couples embrace, friends cheer and slap one another on the back, and longed for simple things; someone to make him a coffee in the morning, someone of whom he could write little messages on the fogged glass of the shower, so she could read them as she bathed. Byrne could smile at others in the crowd, share a mutual excitement at the news that affected all who heard, yet he would still go home alone that night, banking the only human interactions of the day on the few customers he'd received.

By now the captain of the Hobart was sharing a few words, about how 'we should reserve our excitement' and that 'no suitable port could be made' on the shores of the new wintery land, in fact, the towering walls of ice seemed to repel the ship indifferently. The captain had dubbed the landmass Maree-Bird Land, after his ex-wife, for the repellent and cold shores reminded him of her. He laughed awkwardly, and the crowd raised their brows collectively and chuckled back, if only to not be rude. Byrne winced at the comment - were they really going to name such a monumental discovery after the petty squabbles of the man who happened upon it?

"Really selling it, ain't they?" came a voice.

Byrne turned his head to a woman who was leaning her lower back on the counter of his shopfront. Her face was turned to the captain and Libra Tenebrific, so that Byrne could only discern the aquiline profile of her.

"Who? Him or her?"

The woman laughed, "Both."

Her candour broke the ice of awkwardness that had been showered on the crowd, and Byrne was pulled instantly from his quicksand of loneliness.

"Well, I suppose it's a pretty big deal. Although by the sounds, nobody is going to be able to live there,"

The woman turned towards him and stood at full height, and Byrne saw that she was rather taller than he, "It is a big deal. Yet those morons would have you believe they'd merely found a lost watch or figured out the answer to six across."

At this Byrne broke into laughter, and his heart began to race - this happened whenever a woman gave him even the smallest amount of attention. He felt a bead of sweat catch in his greying hair, and hoped to God she hadn't noticed. He was suddenly so conscious of his being - how his squared chin descended into loose neck skin, or how his eyebrows were darker than the hair of his head. *Ridiculous!*

"I'm Byrne,"

The woman winced, "I know, it's written on your sign up there,"

"Uh... yeah, I guess it doesn't matter then."

"Oh, don't admonish yerself," she laughed.

"But what's yours?"

"My what?"

"Name." He said it harsher than intended.

"Don't matter," she said.

Byrne felt his shoulders drop.

"Can I buy this book," here she raised a crimson tome from the countertop, "Maybe I'll really enjoy it. And then come back and buy another book."

"Got plenty of... stuff. Books, I mean,"

Stupid!

She smiled, "See ya Byrne,"

And she was gone, her thick head of hair lost to the steadily dispersing crowd before Byrne could even mention that she'd forgotten to pay. Overwhelmed with a strange exhaustion that descended quickly upon him, Byrne grasped the support propping up the awning of his stall and began to expertly spin it in one hand, round and round until the awning came down, sealing him in momentary darkness. Then, taking hold of his small sack of coins (today's earnings), he locked up shop and wandered back over the Selene Bridge to his home.

The Convent

The bell rang, cutting savagely through the hazy migraine of a warm spring day – it may as well have been summer already. The cicadas mounted their case for chaos with an uproar that threatened to combust and set the forest alight. The strange sound of a school bell just might have been the flint strike to ignite a hot day that was ready to burst. The school itself looked rudely intrusive against the conifer trees that backed it. Situated so pompously in that place where nature claimed rule, it struck down the surrounds with the same oppression that it applied to its students. The Calumnia Convent – where wicked children went to have their youthful exuberance smashed away by a strict regime of 'the ways to do things properly' – it bristled in the aching heat, its sandstone walls contracting from the harsh season that gripped it; the black crows baking from their perch atop the spires. There was method to the madness of its location; any renegade child who thought themselves clever enough to escape would find it impossible to traverse the untidy bushlands beyond, and the school being some ten miles from the nearest township only amplified the danger of desertion. And didn't the teachers of Calumnia know it:

If you fancy yourself as dinner for the Indigo Wolves then you are most welcome to vacate your dorm.

Or –

Now surely a little arithmetic is more inviting than the bite of a Crested Viper?

For every prim hair-bun or neatly clipped moustache of the Convent's teachers there lived the gardeners, the janitors, the undertakers who pruned, swept and waved away the forest from the school grounds and helped maintain that faultless air of superiority. Yes, even nature could not best this school, so why should any student believe *they* themselves could?

On that particular afternoon, at the hour when the sun is at its hottest, the classroom stank of foetid apathy; of teachers whose passion had turned perfunctory, of students who groaned with the awkward pains of growth. Nothing knew its place, and those that claimed otherwise writhed in nomadic denial. A darkness lurked in that room (for the shadows had to hide from the harsh sun somehow), a darkness that sapped the energy from its occupants, while the brightness of daylight blinded them from whatever wonders might lay in wait beyond the window sills. Discomfort swam in the awful headache of the day; could anything break its terrible silence? Could any malady sweat out this fever? The clock hands ticked, the teacher dragged her screeching chalk across the blackboard and from the back row of desks a girl examined the dirt beneath her fingernails. This girl was Delaney Vespers – a child of dark defiance. Her mind a slate, expansive and clean, a canvas awaiting only the most calculated brushstrokes – little else would do.

"Miss Vespers," came a voice.

Shit.

The ambience was broken; Delaney focused her sight and within the crosshairs stood her stout teacher. Despite those prominent proportions, the teacher carried a shrunken and pathetic quality clearly visible through a transparent stance of arbitrary akimbo. Madam Nunwiser stared down through her pince-nez, her nose aquiline – upturned and pretentious. Those eyes of hers seemed emptied of emotion, magnified perhaps by the pince-nez and dried by the spring heat. Delaney's heart sank with defeat; she was an animal cornered by its predator; any swipe in retaliation would be futile. Still though, Madam Nunwiser expected acknowledgement, as such Vespers had little choice but to admit that she had not heard what her superior had said.

"Perhaps, Miss Vespers," Madam said, "if you'd be sure to groom yourself properly, there'd be less to examine beneath those filthy fingernails."

Those behind Madam Nunwiser sniggered while those in front dared not move a muscle. Vespers slouched in defeat – it would be another evening in the kitchens as a dish pig – she knew it. Nunwiser snatched at the paper on Vespers' desk much to the girl's chagrin, and stared down at the little sketches of flying machines scribbled across its surface.

"It surprises me that you are *failing* art as well as history, Miss Vespers," Nunwiser screwed up the drawings in her claw, "Now would you kindly answer my original question?"

Vespers knew what the teacher was doing. She had not been paying attention to the question asked and would have little choice but to humiliate herself by asking for it to be repeated. Madam Nunwiser seemed to pre-empt this and announce in a booming voice, "The fauna of our national emblem, young lady. What are they?"

"The seagull and the big fish,"

"The *Gull* and *Leviathan*, Miss Vespers; you will use their proper titles. And what do these two represent?"

A voice cried from behind her, "It's how the continent came into being, ma'am,"

"Is your name Vespers, Francis?" boomed Madam Nunwiser.

"That's redundant," muttered Vespers.

"Beg pardon, Miss Vespers?"

Vespers cautiously looked up into the teacher's eyes and gained courage as she did so. Could life get any worse? Perhaps not, so she boldly replied, "What you said was redundant. You said his name in the question,"

Madam Nunwiser bristled, "Do not question my grammar, young lady. You'll never become a writer or an artist if you do not heed my lessons."

"But madam," said Vespers, "is the race not long and youth but the outset – why should I learn these things in school? How can you say I will never do such things?"

"What is the meaning of this eloquence? Better for you to apply it to your studies, missy."

"But why? Why language, why mathematics? I won't need it if I'm not allowed to work."

Madam Nunwiser threw her hands up, "I am left with little help to suffer one so wild; be mild, child – your poor husband will appreciate it."

"Why be a poor man's burden? Why must I rely on such an outcome?"

"Naughty knave! Wicked whelp! I should chide you, child! To learn to count, to know value or amount; tis simply the way we do things. You are nothing to question it."

"But,"

"One more word, Miss Vespers; you'll write the doctrine of *Gull and Leviathan* ten times!"

Delaney Vespers slammed her fist on the desk and stood, "No! I won't be some monument! 'The way we do things' – according to whom? I think that you've nothing to support your claims."

The other students giggled nervously through the tension. Delaney stood firm, secretly wishing she'd just kept her mouth shut. Meanwhile Madam Nunwiser stood abashed and wondered how she'd let this situation escalate so.

"Lines, young lady," the teacher boomed, "on my desk tomorrow morning. And you'll spend the rest of the session outside in the halls."

Vespers skulked down the aisle of desks, hating every eye that gawked at her shameful march.

Evening mercifully arrived and soothed the blistered stone buildings of Calumnia, and Delaney Vespers, having herself cooled the brash temper native to her person, lay on her bunk in the dorms and flipped through the pages of lines she had been given as punishment. On hot nights like this the children of the convent were allowed to wander the grounds outside until nine; Vespers hissed in disdain to hear her peers enjoying themselves outside the window. No matter, the mosquitoes would be out in force anyway. Still, those rare nights in the warmer seasons were one of the few reprieves afforded to the students, and even though Vespers yawned with exhaustion she still wished to be free of the dorms. Her rebellious energy had been spent; further reprimanding quashed any further ideas of backchat from her mind. Her hand ached from writing; she had scribed the seventeen stanzas of Gull and Leviathan four times already, and she groaned inwardly to think she was not even halfway through. Curse that Madam Nunwiser! Being such a hot-headed adolescent had given Vespers no advantage in this place, for nobody took a girl of seventeen seriously. There were too few years for her to have garnered the respect she demanded. Yet still Delaney Vespers thought of herself as an old soul – that she had seen it all before, that nothing could surprise her. It was this early development of maturity that had been her curse as her parents (city folk who spoke with more than one plum in their throat) had deemed her ill-mannered and in need of a stint in the harshest boarding school on the continent. The conditions had not suited the young girl from the city; the icy streets had been traded for dry wilderness, and Vespers had not realised that the sun could get quite so hot. She tied her dirty blonde hair and winced – the back of her neck was sweating. The night was so hot that even sitting still seemed to drain one of energy, and she swore through her teeth to observe the smearing of pen ink on her tired hand.

Her thoughts turned to the legendary poem she had been ordered to recite. The Gull and Leviathan held reverence across the continent as a sort of fable; not a creation story per say – rather a haunted life lesson of resilience that the populace held dear. The setting of this great work was what caught Vespers' attention – an icy island on the edge of the world, whose bleak winters sounded more like a sweet relief to her than the barren wasteland they were meant to represent. Delaney Vespers had feigned ignorance to her teacher; she knew the story very well, had seen many incantations of the two protagonists from the continent's national flag to the artworks she'd seen in the museums of the city. To her the seagull and the giant fish had always appeared so disconnected, so foreign that she saw little purpose in learning about them. Surely a text so archaic had no relevance in today's life. Since she was a teenager, anybody older than her was a hypocrite, anyone younger was immature, and nobody struck that sweet balance of maturity and savviness– or at least that's what *she* thought. Still though (and she'd tell no-one of this), there were certain verses of Gull and Leviathan that she found quite pleasant – *why comest thou to me?* – and at that moment, drawn back into the sweltering dorm room, Vespers realised that life was perhaps not as bad as she thought. She would not yield so easily to some uppity teacher who had to suffer the Calumnia life as much as she did. Vespers would not be a trophy of fragility, no ice sculpture; no flower in frost or bird in thunder was she, and one day wouldn't *they* all know it. She'd show them all. It was all about patience – that was one lesson that she had reluctantly learned from her parents – with patience she'd prove her life was one of some value, but what fruits such a life would yield withheld their colours from her at that time.

With the lines of poetry carved deeply into her mind, Delaney Vespers began to write again.

Panjandrum

The Continent of Verdigris may not have had any notable qualities in terms of its perimeter shores – on the maps it was little more than a shapeless blob surrounded by ocean. Yet from shore to shore, north to south, east to west it was brimming with the beauty of nature, the advancements of civilisation and the warmth of life, of connection. There was no other vibrant, or frankly inhabitable place in the world. At the intersection of the four compass points (or one should say, roughly off-centre, for nature is more beautiful without symmetry), its tallest mountain towered above a range of snow-capped peaks. Cardinal Mons, named originally for its central position on the maps, and later for the social status it would imbue, stood tall; sometimes proudly, sometimes ominously, yet soothingly omnipresent. The peak was like an anchor to all who lived on the Continent, immoveable and always there. It snowed year-round near the summit, yet the mountain had a warmth to it, as though it was as alive as the creatures that wandered its slopes, exuding a certain paternal authority over its sovereign lands. And standing proudly on the face of the mountain was the Continent's capital city, in a place where one probably would not expect to find anything at all. It was an old way of thinking – if there were an underworld, then all the better to build a capital at the highest point. A veritable Babel, as it were! Yet there was a further logic to the madness of this snowy locale. The innards and undersides of Cardinal Mons were littered with ice caves; ice caves that housed an exquisite abundance of rainbow crystals that formed there and there alone.

The city was often referred to as one of three titles. For the lower suburbs – those sparser populated streets straddling the precipice of the mountain were collectively called Magna Austere. In the literal sense of the word, the lower class made their homes there, although for a city so opulent it was a rather misleading title. Its locals would prefer comparison to the hard-working citizens of the past who had made the mountain great, living with little luxury for a deserved reward. Still those higher up the slope treated them with a subtle belittlement, and when one from Austere made the trek uphill they'd be dishevelled and flushed from the hike, all the more filling the stereotype that those in Magna Luxuria had blanketed them with. Those from Magna Luxuria knew they sat at the top of the tree. Clung tightly to the battlements of the Governing Manor the houses that lined those streets never fell below three floors in height (the higher the better), and since the weather was cold all year round, the Uppers (as they fashioned themselves) lounged in their baroque homes around marble fireplaces. The citizens were often fat and unseasoned to laborious work; a common joke said that the streets of Luxuria would in time need to be widened to accommodate two people abreast. But they'd clearly done the right things, met the right people and struck the right hot iron – they were by far and away the richest folk of the entire Continent.

The third title of this great city (and indeed the title it was most commonly referred to as) was Magna Austrinus. Easily the largest of those three factions, Austriners were an opaque amalgamation of what the qualities native to both Luxurians and Austerians. Named after the Great South Wind, the title of Magna Austrinus was often confused instead as the 'Great Fish' – many across the Continent erroneously believed this to be a homage to the mighty whale from the lore of *The Gull & Leviathan*, while those not so bright were confused as to why a mountain city was named after a creature of the sea. The peak of that massive mountain, Cardinal Mons, was observable for miles around its base, and glittering near the summit, not to be outdone by the natural zenith, sat the Governing House of Magna Austrinus. It was a garish and beautiful structure; a sort of sick corruption of gothic that had leaked into the decidedly steampunk motives that the city was famous for. Its spires stretched earnestly for ascendancy, and its huge windmills seemed to chip away at the sky itself.

To those who gazed upwards to it, it was a venerable castle in the sky, and on days when the cloud cover hung low the city did in fact appear to float on its own enormous props, spinning lazily in the glacial air. In times past the city had built itself on the morals of its motto – *'those who toil shall be lifted'* – the high altitude and snow-struck climate meant only the hardiest survived those early days of the city's infancy. Over the years its elevated position and opulent populace meant that such promises of hard work rewarded were left unrecognised; to be born in Austrinus would usually mean one remained in Austrinus, for there was, quite literally, no higher place to live. As such generations of its inhabitants grew fat with arrogance; all the rail tracks led to Austrinus, and it would forever be the capital of the continent and the seat of power – no other settlement came close. Given its cramped streets the residents would rarely venture far, and the lack of suitable farmlands in the mountains meant that the city survived off of the imports from the continent's *richer* soils. Richer, it could be said with a demeaning chuckle, for the gem stones that were the major export of Austrinus were valued above all other currency across the continent. They were the very reason the city had been settled in the first place. Yes, so long as they kept taunting those 'lower' with coloured gems, the food and coal would keep flowing toward them.

Lo! To describe the shimmering beauty of the residents, each of whom wore their status with a pomp attitude and dressed themselves like one more bauble on a garish Christmas tree. The women, preened to perfection like so many birds-of-paradise, smelling of scented oils whose fragrances settled on fur hats and colourful scarves. While the men would strut, peacock-proud with coats and shoes of a sharp black, their vests as fabulous as Faberge eggs while they smoked their pipes, smoothed their beards and made inquiries to their golden pocket watches on *'what the time might be'*. Everyone was busy being busy, and to claim otherwise simply wouldn't do. There were profits to be counted – each day the miners would return to their masters with their latest haul, while the city alchemists conjured ways to produce minerals to an endless amount. Perhaps the people of Austrinus were in fact blinded by colour (were such a thing possible), for everywhere was an assault to the eyes and cloaked the greedy gazers from the possibility of a darker future – *those who toil shall be lifted!* Why would that ever change?

There were others, however, who were not so lucky. Not that they'd know it though; Pan, Jan and Drum, three bumbling city officials, exerted their best efforts into the *very* important tasks laid out for them. It is said that there is 'one in every family' – referring to the so-called black sheep, figures cut of the same cloth as others more opulent but alas, cast to the cutting room floor, and in this particular case there were three. These three brothers were well-meaning in a way, but exuded a moronic arrogance that came across as bombastic. Their parents had been a hardworking count and countess who had sowed their youth and freedom on the icy slopes and reaped a harvest of fantastic fortune. If all children ended up like their parents, then Pan, Jan and Drum would be set. Unfortunately for the count and countess, their offspring never quite caught hold of the concepts of mining gems, of counting profits or even basic hygiene. Whispers fluttered on the social winds that perhaps the triplets had been left out in the cold at a young age and had stunted their development as a result. But such a claim is perhaps too cruel to say, for the boys had no issue with the simpler vocations dumped upon them. Vocations that, given the snobbery of Austrinus residents, nobody else could suffer undertaking. There they were, one faceless Monday morning, standing before the enormous clock that marked the centre of Austrinus central business district. It was an elaborate network of cogs and metronomes, glistening in the crisp early sunlight in wondrous shimmers of chrome and brass. It was a masterpiece of engineering and the pride of Magna Austrinus, to look upon it was to observe not only the time, star date or season but to also be reminded to keep one's nose up, because *'those who toil shall be lifted!'* and those who wasted *time* were doomed to fail.

"Here it comes again! Grab hold, Pan!"

The second hand of the great clock slid slowly down toward them; sickle sharp but with an arrowhead-like tip that provided decent enough foothold to jump aboard.

"Pan, I say! Grab hold!"

"Brother," came the response, "you are Pan. I am Jan."

"Quiet, Drum. I was speaking to Pan."

"No, I am Drum. Did you think I was Jan?"

"Who is Pan? You think I am?"

"Did you say Jan? – Oh! Too slow!"

The minute swung past six and begun its ascent back to twelve. Another minute wasted. Pan, who had been at fault in the first place, dealt a pitiful backhand across the faces of his brothers.

"Fools! We'll never clean this clock at this rate!" he cried.

"Are you sure Lady Tenebrific would have us clean it this way?" piped Drum.

"Well, the clock hand already knocked the ladder over, and you see how high it goes!" said Jan.

"I just think there must be an easier way to scrub up at twelve..."

Pan threw his chest out, "Clearly Libra intended for *me* to lead this task! You numpties have no clue!"

"Shouldn't call Lady Tenebrific so... 'tis disrespectful."

"If you did so, perhaps," said Pan, "but the Miss Libra and I are, shall we say, on a par? She..."

"Clock hand again." Drum interrupted.

"Well don't just stand there."

Poor Jan (who Pan assumed was Drum) snatched up his sodden sponge and watched the clock hand arrive level with him. The suds made his hand cold, and slippery to boot; already he had fallen from clock's pinnacle twice that morning. Still, with the fearlessness that comes only with ignorance, he leapt up in a rather maladroit fashion and clung desperately to the brass needle hand. Up, up he went, past nine - from there things got tricky. Steadying himself with one arm hugged to the clock hand he tipped himself upright whilst pressing the sponge to the clock face as he spun, leaving a soapy smear in its wake. In honesty the clock was not even in need of cleaning; that job was usually undertaken by the tower man, who performed a far more sensible job too. As the hand once again began its descent, from the throat of the clock came an almighty bell call that rung in the ninth hour of the morning. The vibration that sung through the brass hands sent Jan's equilibrium into chaos and the poor fool tumbled to the ground and landed heavily on his foot.

"Typical ignorance, Drum!" cried Pan.

"I don't think we're doing it right," whimpered the real Drum.

"Nonsense, Pan! Miss Libra made it quite clear that she wanted to 'clean my clock' – and do you *see* any other clock around here?"

"I think my foot is broken..." said Jan.

Pan ignored his poor brother and stood with arms akimbo, admiring what he would call *a good morning's work*.

"Well, it's clear of snow, and by gar it looks good in the morning sun. Job done, boys!"

"What about the ladder?" asked Drum.

"An unfortunate casualty,"

"Don't wanna report to Lady Tenebrific; she frightens me,"

"I can't walk...," cried Jan.

Pan huffed impatiently and turned to Drum, "Jan, help brother Pan!"

Confused and battered, Drum helped Jan to his feet. Pan had already begun a proud saunter up the main boulevard towards the manor. His brothers sulked in his trail.

"Don't know why you get to boss us around..."

"Because, boys," replied Pan, "I am the eldest by a good two minutes! Count 'em, watch that clock if you please! Har har, the ignorance, indeed!"

The Incumbent & the Challenger

Those who toil shall be lifted – the motto of Magna Austrinus was never far from the minds of its citizens, yet a certain changing of the guard had seeped beneath the cracks in the floor of recent times, rising slowly like smoke into the attitudes of many. A new colour was being mixed onto the palette, and just when society appeared weary of the same tones of banality this colour struck them with the force of wonderful anticipation – of change that would usher in glory. Magna Austrinus was well-established; the hard work had been done. Was it not time to enjoy the fruits that blossomed from the old generation's hardships? Was now not the time to lift ancient families up - not on a foundation of mud and brick, but rather the abundance of wealth that poured upon that fertile land? The woman who had led this revolution remained in charge of the entire Continent after several years of prosperity. Her reign had brought with it these drastic changes to the very fabric on which all previous ways had been stitched. She was the Lady Libra Tenebrific.

As a woman built on luxury, when Libra Tenebrific entered a room, she filled it. She carried her massively fat body with an aura of grandeur, dusky curls spewing from the top of her head like the lava flow of a volcano. Although she only chose to move when she had to, there was a slow and languid grace to her movements that many found hypnotic. Oft times her face would tell an entire story in one expression, be it a cold and heartless stare (a gaze that could make anybody reconsider opposing her) or the hint of a smile from the upturned corners of the lips – a look that gave her an air of unshakeable confidence. She was all things beauty in a woman, albeit exaggerated to their most extreme limits. Her hedonistic surfeits left her overripe, like fruit left on the branch for a day too long. Not wont to be denied in any account, the very air around Lady Libra felt heavy, and her lifestyle was sick with sweet excess.

Her past was shrouded in mystery; Libra claimed to have emerged from a *great darkness*, although exactly what that meant she would say very little more. Like most officials she had a knack for talking her way out of any situation, which only added to her appeal among the voting public of Verdigris. Surely there were few who could possibly like her on a personal level (her remarkable arrogance saw to that, and oppressed maid servants could attest), but her leadership skills had been the perfect tonic for the current age. Others questioned how one so young could possess such impressive skills, for she appeared as one perhaps in her mid-thirties, but spoke like one much more advanced and worldlier. For the first time in the remaining recorded history a woman held the highest echelon of leadership; whether a citizen liked her or not, Libra's influence could not be understated. The world appeared to be more self-absorbed by the minute, partaking to the inward-looking human nature or not. Libra was the perfect pin-up for such an attitude. *Let them eat cake* – a long lost proverb whose true meaning was lost to the ages - was perhaps an appropriate catch-cry, for it was abundantly clear that Libra had her cake and ate it too.

If she had but one weakness, it was this hopeless affliction to gluttony. As her ego was fed on accolades so too did Libra indulge on her obsession – what she would call *one innocent little vice*. The high life had been kind to the senses, lavish in its offerings, and Lady Libra had worked far too hard obtaining such status as to deny herself *just one more slice of pie*. More could never be enough, and how wonderful it felt to be *big*. She was a big deal, the biggest deal across the entire

Continent. If anyone stood before her and she'd take them down.

There she sat before her vanity, the stool on which she ensconced vanishing beneath her enormous bottom and swathes of her absurdly tight dress of charcoal-coloured satin. Here a groan could be heard as she shifted her weight from one buttock to another, confirming that the chair still toiled under her. There joining the struggle – the creak of seams straining to contain her immensity. She preened at furtive lashes, pruned at striking brows and dressed her pale face like some glorious bird of paradise. Her chambers were deathly quiet, and Libra relished the silence of the morning, knowing that it was not to last much longer. The curtains were drawn closed – Libra was one who valued her beauty sleep, and the harsh light of dawn was something that one must slowly become accustomed to as the day progressed. She turned to the doors – mighty oak things carved exquisitely with gothic ornament – and gazed shiftlessly through the oceanic void. Perhaps she hadn't heard anything at all.

But she had heard something. Yes, there was no denying the sound of that maladroit gait – Polly Jean Cupio, Libra's chief maidservant, would soon enter the room. Libra squeezed her amber eyes shut and waited impatiently for what she knew would follow. There it was – a timid knock at the oak doors that insulted their impressiveness with its lack of surety.

"Yes," sighed Libra.

The door opened, and Miss Cupio tottered in on vacillating legs, dragging behind her a trolley of breakfast foods and newspapers. Just as Libra had anticipated this exact entrance, Polly Jean knew too that Libra would tell her that she 'didn't have to knock every time', but this was a lie she would not put her faith in. The last time Polly had entered unbidden she had received quite the verbal tirade for intruding on Libra's personal space. No, she'd never risk it again!

"Shall I let some light in, miss?" asked Miss Cupio, trying to avoid those cat-like eyes of Libra that stared so intimidatingly at her through the gloom.

"I suppose it's time, yes," Libra sighed, "I can't chase *this* day away,"

"Oh, don't be upset, it will be fine,"

Libra winced irritably as the morning sun spilled into her chamber; a huge four-post bed lay unmade against one wall that dwarfed the opulence of the rest of the room. Libra's many lovely possessions were all contained in this one room, for she refused to share anything she considered valuable, and Polly Jean could never help but gasp at the beauty of these luxurious trinkets. Libra's library took up another wall, and more books lay scattered about the floor; a large sepia globe gathered dust in another corner, and her wardrobe was an organised chaos of clothing of epic variety and proportion. Atop her vanity – a disorderly shamble of perfumes and jewellery, each piece placed exactly where *she* intended. Her way or no way; this was the mantra of Lady Libra Tenebrific, from her career right down to the smaller details of life that others might not pay so much attention to. She brushed a strand of hair from her face and held out the other hand expectantly. Polly Jean duly placed a small pastry in that palm and proceeded to pour coffee from a large urn that was a bit too much for her emaciated arms to handle. In her haste to not spill its contents and evoke Libra's wrath she steadied it with one hand, wincing at the immediate scalding that ensued. Polly gritted her teeth and brushed the pain onto her smock; no matter, the urn remained upright and Libra was calm – worth it for a small injury. In fact, Lady Tenebrific had not noticed her antics at all, instead clasping another pastry (for the first was swiftly devoured) and reading the newspaper vehemently. Like an actress awaiting her first review, Libra always approached the papers with a schoolgirl eagerness – any mention of her name only inflated her ego further and she lavished any attention, provided it remained positive. Should any writer decide that there was some issue with her, well, let it be said that their days of dipping pen into inkpots were numbered. Her eyes raced over the front page and soon narrowed.

"Why there is no mention of me at all! And on the front page! Potential pandemic, miners falling ill, what is all this?"

"Oh, I wouldn't worry, miss. There's plenty on how *bad* Spindle is. Here, you should eat,"

Polly handed over another pastry which Libra absently stuffed betwixt her lips, "Well I hardly need the papers to dish up dirt on Spindle. The man sabotages himself with his ignorance. What are they saying?"

"That he lacks charisma," replied Polly, "pie?"

Libra nodded, "A halfwit could deduce that; he's as fun as cold porridge. No, it's this lack of focus on me that is concerning. I need to remain relevant in the public eye. They need to know I'm the one who gave them such fine lifestyle,"

Polly Jean began to fold some of the clothing that Libra had left discarded on the floor. Outside the clock in the Central District rung solemnly.

"That reminds me, miss," said Miss Cupio, "the Drum boys finished cleaning the clock; Jan – or at least I think it was Jan – he's broken his foot."

"Ugh, you bring this up now?"

"W-what should I tell them?"

Libra moved to slam her fist on the vanity, before catching herself at the last moment, "I don't care, just keep them out of my sight!"

Polly Jean started to feel a little scared; Libra's temper was remarkably short, and she knew one wrong move here would send her into a frenzy. That was bad news for all who dwelled in Government House, for Libra's fits of fury were famous for dampening the mood of the entire populace of servants. To deflect these volleys was Miss Cupio's main task, but she also disliked seeing her superior in bad spirits. Despite the obvious short fallings in Libra's persona, Polly Jean saw past that and instead channelled her unfulfilled ambitions into the woman she answered to daily. Whether she did this purposefully or not was known only to her, but it seemed that Miss Cupio dreamed of being even half as successful as Libra had been; in a way, she coveted the gourmand.

"Not to worry, miss. Mr. Spindle is defeating himself in this campaign. You just need to keep up appearances and it's a sure thing. Here, eat more."

"You are impossibly stupid sometimes, Polly," sighed Libra, "you all are. But I suppose you are right this one time."

****

Until recently, one question had carried itself through the city with feverish intensity. Who is this Spindle? What could be said of him? For starters, the man stood as Libra's opponent in the upcoming electoral campaign. If Libra Tenebrific was of looks more youthful than expected, then Spindle was quite the opposite. Despite an emaciated frame, his shoulders slouched as though they had burdened an immense weight, and he possessed an empty grey stare that told of sorrows a thousandfold. To strike his rib one might expect to hear the humourous tone of a xylophone, so comical was his stature. His hair had begun to recede before its time, turned white as the snows of Cardinal Mons and deathly-looking as dried grass readying for kindling. While Libra could leave one feeling a rather vicarious repletion, Spindle served a barren meal for the mind, and those who listened to his speech would feel empty and wanting. He was tall, but so jaded of posture that he seemed smaller; everything about the man was an ebbing tide.

Like Libra he had emerged as if from nowhere, however Spindle's was a story far less romanticised. His was a thankless upbringing, but not one he would trade off for anything. Austin Spindle had quietly lived the entirety of his years in Magna Austere, hence embodying that stoic attitude of the older generation, an attitude that he had shoved closer toward self-depravity. This was his pride and trophy; *he* knew the results of forbearance that the opulent city of Magna

Austrinus had forgotten. It was *his* determination to preserve the old way of thinking that would lead the Continent into a new age of prosperity... Eventually.

Yes, if only they'd see. If only they'd remove their pince-nez and dirty their hands, then they'd see how the great city had become as such in the first place!

Spindle's father would be so proud!

But then again one must not allow oneself to become conceited.

There was still work to be done, an election to win and, all puns intended, he was battling with the heavyweight now. Now any healthy competition is usually flourished with just a little spite, however Austin Spindle's distaste for Libra had verged onto utter disdain. Quite simply, he despised her. Despised her arrogance, despised the insular attitude she had instilled in the great city's increasingly selfish citizens. Throughout his campaign he had remained in his meagre home in the suburbs of Austere, despite the regular formality that saw the opposition leader reside in the 'Opponent's Wing' of Government House for the duration of the election preceding. Spindle could claim that his decision to live a life less opulent was a vain attempt to see less of Lady Libra; there may indeed have been truth in that, but he would pronounce he was *living amongst the people,* something he hoped might convince others of his potential as leader. Truth be told it was mostly because he hated change, and being so set in his ways he found it difficult to alter even the smaller nuisances of his pedantic life.

Pedantry practiced to a fault; such was the ways of Austin Spindle, who sat before his rather grimy mirror and huffed, flummoxed at the wet reed of grey hair on his head that refused to fall into line. There was no need to give visitors a grand tour of his abode, for it was all there to be seen as soon as one entered the door. Being built on the face of a mountain had its limitations, and the great city of Magna Austrinus, although not lacking in size, had many of its homesteads crammed together, built on top of one another, and brushed uncomfortably close to the neighbours. Like penguins huddling for warmth did those buildings stand, and Spindle's home was a one-room apartment situated above and below other homes of the same layout. He could offer you little, not for lack of wealth but through prudent living. Say you were chilled to the bone after traipsing through the streets of Austere – a hot cup of coffee or tea would be a most welcome elixir. Spindle could offer you such a beverage, albeit watered down immensely so as to save on his supply of the stuff, and there would be little doubt in him serving up a tepid drink, as boiling water used precious energy that *he* must pay for. For food – impossibly hard bread bordering stale, with perhaps a scrape of butter if he was feeling generous. These anti-social tendencies seemed normal to him; yet as one who could not see the forest for the trees, he did not notice the discomfort he placed upon others.

The chief advisor of the opposition leader, young Silas, knew of all these strange behaviours and was far more tolerant of them than many others had been in his oft friendless life. Then again, he had never become expectant of very much, having been stunted in the legs since birth and confined to a wheelchair ever since. Silas was an upbeat but easily downtrodden man, and although he never expressed anger or frustration consciously, it was often written in his twitchy movements – the sweat on his narrow brow, the lenses of his glasses fogged up with irritation. There was surprising strength in those thin arms of his, forced to propel his wheelchair as other bipeds used their legs, but when he had entered one of these frustrated moods, his palms would sweat, and any attempt to remove himself from the issue were foiled by them slipping off the wheels of his chair. So, despite the infuriating repetition of Spindle's preening of his wayward hair, and his metronomic utterance of "my most amiable fellows," Silas would not let himself get heated.

"*My most amiable fellows,*" Spindle said again, "is that a good opener, Silas?"

Silas adorned a face of obedience, "Why yes, sir. I believe that is well said. Might I suggest you use the gel, sir?"

"The tube is empty," Spindle fumed, "and still this rotten hair of mine!"

"If I may, sir,"

Silas wheeled over and offered a comb from his pocket, before returning to the single wooden table Spindle possessed in his home. It was littered with papers.

"*My most amiable fellows...* Too proper? How about – *hello dudes and chicks?*"

"*Dudes and chicks*, sir?" Silas tried to suppress his laughter.

"Well, that's what people say, is it not?"

Austin Spindle had failed and given up altogether on his hair and now struggled with the beige tie he had planned to wear with his neatly ironed white shirt.

"Uh, stick with the first one...," said Silas.

"Hmm, maybe. But perhaps leave the speech to me, Silas. After all, I am the one giving it."

"Don't you have a more... Punchy colour, sir?" asked Silas, gazing at the neck tie.

Spindle's hands convulsed with the irritation of tying a difficult knot, "What? What's wrong with this one? Beige! Neutral! A colour of purity! Anybody can relate to it!"

"If you say so, sir."

"I do. And it offends nobody."

The window frame rattled with an unexpected gust that drew Spindle towards it. Fortune had favoured him in this one sense; his apartment happened to face southward and given the sloping nature of the city this afforded him a spectacular view of the mountains that crowded Cardinal Mons. Every jutting peak and crestfallen valley sparkled with the morning sunlight that reflected off last night's snowfall. Spindle surveyed this domain – a domain he hoped to rule over in due time. Behind him, Silas sifted through newspapers and furrowed his brow in an attempt to gain his master's attention. He would not like what he had to say, and as such Silas dithered and danced around the elephant in the room that was printed in large black letters. He would be relieved of any confronting statement by Spindle turning with a sigh and addressing him, "So how bad can it be?"

Silas winced and slid the paper across the table towards him, "Not bad, so to say. This seems more focussed on the rumblings of an illness contracted by the miners. As for you, it's just that the public find you lack a little charisma."

Austin Spindle snorted and laughed loudly, although anyone who heard it would know for certain that it was forced – the opposition leader was a renowned humourless character. Yes, Silas knew that laugh; knew that it concealed an irate insecurity dressed as bewilderment.

Lacking charisma indeed, Ha!

The opposition leader clapped his advisor on the back, insipid frustration disguised as confidence. Each belittling pat on Silas' back replenished Spindle's lagging confidence; there was a debate happening shortly, and now was the time for him to make a stance. They wanted charisma? He could manage that, surely. After all, he'd focussed his entire life upon achievement through atonement, this was just one more obstacle to summit.

"No matter, boy!"

Silas hated being referred to as 'boy'. Yet again he refused to correct him for fear of confrontation, instead quipping, "Perhaps we should be on our way, sir."

Spindle puffed his chest out proudly, "Why yes, Silas. Time we hit the ground running! Now what are you looking at me like that for?"

On the Train to Banksia

By the time mid-morning had rolled around the locomotive had built up a good head of steam, and its sleek burgundy engine shone in the sunlight. Mornings were always cool on the mountain range in which the train chuffed through, around and under; even in the warmer months. The gale that blew off Cardinal Mons reached a considerable radius that reminded the passengers of its omnipotence long after the train had pulled out from the central station of Magna Austrinus. The mist had cleared to reveal the beauty of the countryside – pines clambered atop one another up and down the valleys; the train had passed that unseen line where taller trees struggled to grow in the cold. Here and there an icy brook would cascade down black stone cliffs and trickle verdantly into the highland farms. Older folk had called this part of the Continent 'the land of the crooked crop', given the wheat that grew up and down the range appeared to slant sideways. This, of course, was hardly as unique as they may have believed, for gravity said that the grass would grow up, regardless of topography. But such things were a magic mystery that surely couldn't be real – for there were modern men and women who proposed that the earth was round! Round! Of all things!

Well, how do we not roll right off the planet? The old thinkers would quip.

Such thoughts would not concern the passengers on Locomotive 1412 that morning; no, they simply stared out the windows, admiring the beauty, or busied themselves with the newspaper crossword, lulled by the contentedness afforded by the rhythmic *rush-rush-rush* of the wheels turning or the *thumpa-dump thumpa-dump* of the rattling carriages. Not all would be hushed by that locomotive lullaby, however, as one man in particular tried to ignore the gaze of a certain haggard geriatric that had seated himself within eyesight at the other end of the empty carriage.

There is one on every train, he thought, *and today he has chosen to pester me.*

The younger man (not the *young* man, yet he was a generation behind the old hobo sitting across from him) had intentionally chosen this carriage for its lack of passengers, hoping for a moment's respite from the grief that plagued him. Vitus was his name, and he had just paid visit to Magna Austrinus on unfortunate business – his father had passed away. Unmarried and entering the fifth decade of his life, Vitus was beginning to feel as though isolation was his burden to carry. His mother still lingered in the world, albeit hopelessly stricken by madness, and his father had long been out of the picture up until his death, having suffered a breakdown of his marriage and making a new life in the mines of Cardinal Mons. Vitus hated himself for his thoughts – primarily what he deemed a 'selfish' sense of relief at having been to his father's funeral, over at last, and now beginning the journey back to his hometown of Banksia. As with all avenues of closure he had seen the funeral as a turning of a new page in the journey through grief, and perhaps he was a step closer to feeling normal again. But then what? His sister had fortuned far better than he; happy to settle with a young Banksian man and raise her children on the coast. Vitus never spited his sister for that yet felt like he himself could have done something a bit less ordinary with his life. Here he was though, early-forties and devoid of that 'something' he thought would have come to him by now.

I should have married Valerie, he thought then, for no reason in particular.

Like all pivotal moments in his life though, Valerie was long out of the picture. His schoolyard romance with her seemed like another world ago. Just the same was his strained relationship with his deceased father. If only he'd been more open to his dad's interests instead of painting him as some ogre; well, it was too late to fix that! Now nothing 'pivotal' ever seemed to happen.

Now you're just feeling sorry for yourself. Get over it, Vitus.

He saw similarities between his racing thoughts and the racing train. Life was just a big long marathon, and when it came down to it, he was the only one competing. Grief was a beast that struck when it pleased, so Vitus would relish the sudden turn in his persona towards closure and acceptance.

But that's being ruined by this old coot who won't stop staring at me!

Vitus often felt himself akin to a snow globe. Mild when still but rattle him up and it took him a while to become calm. And now he continued his self-depreciating thoughts bemoaning that his solitude had been interrupted. Sure, this old guy was entitled to a seat on the train as much as he (although Vitus doubted the man's ability to pay up a few grubby coins), but did he have to bother him so? The old man, seemingly realising that Vitus' thoughts had drifted to him, rose up from his seat and shuffled his way over, before plonking down opposite the chagrin Vitus.

"Say there, mate," he began.

"No," fumed Vitus, "sorry but no. I don't have any spare change. Not today, nope."

The old man laughed in a surprisingly good humour, his spittle flying from his rotted mouth in wheezing chuckles, "Why friend, I was merely wanting to say – the refreshment lady gave me two sandwiches for the price of one! Said they'd be going bad otherwise. Wanted to offer you one!"

Nice one, arsehole, Vitus berated himself, *he's actually a good guy.*

"Oh," Vitus was not sure how to respond; he certainly didn't feel right taking from a man he'd just insulted, even if he had offered willingly, "Look I'm sorry, guy. I shouldn't have…"

"So, who'll win?" the old man cut him off.

"What?"

"The election! Who'll win?"

Ah, so that's his game, thought Vitus, *but where's the tin-foil hat?*

"I… I don't care much for politics."

"Ah but you should," said the old man, "Me though? Maybe I should stop caring. Lord knows I probably won't live that much longer for it to matter."

"Morbid," quipped Vitus, "but a funny thought."

"I'm Galimatias!"

"You don't say,"

"No, me name! Yowie Galimatias!"

"Ironic,"

"Yep, heard that before,"

Vitus turned to face the window, hoping that Mr. Galimatias would get the picture and leave him alone. He squeezed his eyes shut and scratched the stubble on his chin; he knew Yowie was still looking at him.

"I had black hair like yours once," said Yowie, "back when nobody thought a woman would ever lead the Continent! Har!"

Growing evermore impatiently, Vitus coughed awkwardly. He knew he should probably stand up for womenfolk; his sister would fume at comments like that. But Vitus was a coward; he knew it. Never willing to rock the boat or rebuke someone else's opinion.

Or tell another man to leave him alone.

"Can't say the other bloke is much to write home about though," muttered Yowie.

Accepting his fate, Vitus opened his mouth, "They're chalk and cheese."

Masticating on his sandwich in that awful way older men are wont to do, Yowie's eyes widened, and he hurriedly swallowed his mashed-up snack. He'd gotten a bite, had old Yowie; the line had been still for hours but now he'd gotten a bite.

"Completely!" he burst, "That big fat woman – what's her name – *Tenebrific*, that's it! A hedonist on all fronts! But where do the riches come from if we all of us ain't pitchin' in!"

With that incoherent gem old man Yowie reached into his swag and removed a half-empty bottle of spirits.

"Ye'll have to 'scuse me," he took a swig, "bit of a vampire for the old drink."

"That's ok," Vitus lied, although the reek of booze was *slightly* more tolerable than the smell of that damned sandwich.

"Yet Spindle," continued Yowie, "Yer couldn't thread a needle through his clacker! He's tight I'll tell ya. And take it from an old bastard who's seen the top and twenty k's south of rock bottom – money ain't worth squat if it's scrooged away."

"Scrooged?"

"Scrooged! Spindle gets in and he'll just sit there and 'protect' the economy. Well, all he's really gun be doing is warming his backside on our hard-earned cash!"

Vitus doubted that the old man was contributing much *hard-earned cash*, but he'd been wrong about him already. That, and the train was only an hour or so away from the next stop, and maybe the old man would get off.

"Some are arguing that Libra Tenebrific is doing the same thing."

"Aye, and it's quite a lot of backside that needs a warming. Y'ask me it's an election nobody wants. Who d'ye vote for when they's both horrible?"

I didn't ask you, thought Vitus, *ah! Why is Banksia the last stop?*

"So, what's your spiel? Where ye from? Where ye going?"

"Banksia," said Vitus, "came from the Mons. My old man; he uh, he died."

Yowie crossed himself, "Ah, too sorry, friend. Losing a father is a tough thing."

What would you know, you old reptile?

Vitus would again berate himself; this old man would have had a father once. Perhaps he'd been dead a while, yet Yowie would have still suffered what Vitus was experiencing now at one stage or another.

"Banksia, though," continued Yowie, "a fine place; ain't seen it in years h'ever. Saw a new year show there once – long ago though. The fireworks are probably a lot more elaborate these days."

Any further colloquy from Yowie would be intercepted by the arrival of a train guard who wandered down the central aisle and the old man, never being one to avoid a good chin-wag with any fellow, halted the guard and begun to blather anew. Vitus was at last able to enjoy a moment to himself, and turned his thoughts to his hometown of Banksia. He had forever known it as a haven, the most perfectly unique village on the south-west coast. The nostalgia of a happy childhood veiled its inadequacies, and despite the lofty ambitions he had foreseen himself fulfilling, Banksia was always the backdrop of that success. The village, were it proper to title itself as such, took its name from the Water Banksia – a variant of mangrove tree that grew not on solid ground, on *terra firma*, but instead sprouted from the salty shallows of swamp that morphed into the sea with no tangible shoreline. Those banksia cones were a symbol of the water-rich region in which they grew, and shared their branches with the houses of the Vitus' hometown. Banksia was, in a literal sense, a city raised from the earth; the sturdy wood of the mangroves carved into boardwalks and homesteads and held above the high tide of swamp in the nurturing branches of the trees from whence they'd grown. It was a most unusual construction, yet its foundations had long petrified to become impossibly tough; not even the annual king tide or occasional cyclonic weather was enough to knock the town of Banksia from its perch. By nightfall the swamp lit up with a splendid phosphorescent, brought about by the strange behaviour of the marine life that lived in the shallows below the boardwalks. There was little need for streetlamps because of this – the weedy sea dragons and penta-starfish glowed with a magnificent blue-green hue, a property that higher minds attributed as some form of communication amongst the species. The whole effect gave Banksia a nightly light show and covered the inhabitants with an ethereal sense of peace, and Banksians were a peaceful if not isolated folk.

To be home! Such thoughts that fill the maudlin wanderer anon swam bittersweet from heart to soul for the Banksian man named Vitus. The bleak cold that radiated with raw abandon from Cardinal Mons had been a cruel shock to his system. He had never seen the snow until his father's funeral, and unlike others who seemingly return to childhood at the very sight of those winter flakes, Vitus instead yearned for his humid homestead. His bones were not used to the sorrowful season that is winter and he felt more productive, more malleable in a warmer climate.

I'll never understand how father tolerated such a sea change, Vitus thought, *hmm — sea change. How droll. I won't be needing this coat anymore I suppose.*

His thought train would be derailed, so to say, by a sudden lurching movement that brought the locomotive to a grinding halt.

"Fuck bugger me!" cried the old man Yowie, who had been thrown into the train guard by the impact.

The steam train had come to a standstill upon a winding cliff face and, giving the suddenness of its stopping, was perhaps fortunate to have not been knocked from the rails in the process. To one side the stony cliff face greeted spectators while the jagged tops of the conifers dominated the other side with their saw-toothed canopy.

"Gentlemen, are you alright?" came the voice of the guard.

"Sweet Lord JC! Think I'll be fine," Yowie swore.

"I'll be ok," replied Vitus, "but sir, you aren't looking well."

Indeed, the train guard was visibly hurting, clutching at a shoulder. Stoic to his station, he maintained his facade of professionalism, and informed them that he would inquire about the disturbance. Turning to leave he was approached by another train guard and the two muttered to each other in a low volume. Unable to help himself, Vitus piqued his ears to their tête-à-tête, and felt less guilty to see Yowie was doing the same.

"... We've hit something..." Vitus heard.

And – "Is there a zoologist aboard?"

"... No injuries to passengers, it would seem..."

"... Unlike any *creature* I've ever seen before..."

Vitus, who hitherto could have been blamed for dwelling on the past, had been hauled into the present; his heart feeling decided unease from the clandestine palaver of the train guards and the inevitable delay that the train's incident would cause. Yowie Galimatias had once again seated himself opposite Vitus and presently swigged at his bottle of spirits.

"Better get comfortable, my boy. We're still a long way from Banksia."

The Woodnote Boys

It rained most of the time on the Norfolk Shore. Rheneas Woodnote, having spent his childhood in that temperate cove, was growing up with more downpours to his name than sun beams, and knowing no better meant that he had accepted his truth of nature as gospel. The Woodnote family, living in a sandstone house nondescript from all the other homesteads in Norfolk, lived by and for the sea. On days when the clouds would part, and a deep blue sky shone over the hilly crescent of the bay, the villagers would breathe deep of the outside air and glorify the beauty of their homes. As if making up for lost time the sun shone fiercely on those days it was permitted, and threw its rainbows through the veil of recent rain and sea spray. The Norfolk pines outnumbered all else, revered as sylvan guardians towering over the township where the fishermen cast their nets like maids making the beds, hauling their slumberous catch from the lazy waters until their arms ached and their biceps bulged. There was nothing special about the Woodnote family; Rheneas and his brother Balfour were well aware of their father's simple station, but that did not stop them from fearing their ma and da with that unquestionable respect native to good boys who would become good men. Their da worked the nets with no unique talent, and he expected no reward from his work other than a humble pay cheque and the satisfaction of helping his hometown economy.

A simple lifestyle painted a picture of serene tranquillity, and so it was that the nomads who passed through that part of the coast were surprised to hear of a peculiar phenomenon that had tarred the Norfolkians with a suspicious brush. For your average vagabond would knock back his schooner at the tavern and listen to the loquacious locals speak of spirits that roamed the conifer-cloaked hills. The wanderers, who more often than not practiced no grounded faith, might chuckle inwardly at what they deemed paranoid simpletons whose sheltered life was holding them back from divine knowledge. *They* had travelled this vast continent; *they* had seen what lay beyond the pines; perhaps you Norfolkians ought to step back and 'see the forest for the trees' as it were. But the locals would not be moved; it was true – the

Norfolk Wights traipsed the hills on clear nights when the moon shone a certain way. Their ghostly hoods could be seen ascending the hills in a metronomic line, their faces always hidden from view, cast to the ground beneath their feet, their faith wholly placed in the lanterns they held before them. Everyone knew of the ghosts; when their androgynous forms were spied by the night watchman the locals would bunker down inside their houses and await the dawn. Given the arrival of the spectres only on nights where rain fell not, it was rare to see a Norfolkian on the streets at night, and other cultures around the continent had taken to mocking them for 'being 'fraid o' the dark'.

Norfolk, Norfolk,

I ain't spinning you no joke,

They shake with tail betwixt their legs

And to the ghosts for dawn they begs!

It was observed that the Norfolk Wights only ever ascended the hills; once cresting the summit they would disappear from view, while a new apparition arose as if from the base of the incline and begun its own journey uphill. Why then did the locals quiver so at the sight of these beings? Some rumbled of an ancient tomb buried beneath the hills, while others claimed that the Wights were a metaphor for sinful villagers in need of atonement. One thing was for certain; no man ever approached the ghosts and returned to tell the story. There were a few who claimed to have approached the hills to examine the nocturnal visage, but like fog the ghosts would vanish when one drew close, and all that remained was a soft and ominous chanting. One might have ideas of the crazed town drunk who'd seen the ghosts and returned to swap stories for beer, but no. This was not the typecast ghost story; no-one claimed ownership of the phenomenon. The locals would simply have nothing to do with it, *if ye wanna gallivant off chasing ghosts then be my guest.*

Rheneas and Balfour, being curious boys that they were, heard stories of the Wights with a delightful awe. In particular Rheneas, who preferred the indoors somewhat more than his brother, soaked in any tale that had the hint of macabre; folk at the library knew him well, for he would bury his head into any horror story with vigour. He was a boy of too many skills, none of which he could claim to be a budding master, and his ma would often tell him to *slow down 'afore he hurt himself.* Indeed Rheneas brimmed with a skittish energy; he crammed far too much into his mind to function at times. But he liked it that way – Lord gave him a brain, he may as well use it. As for Balfour, well he had accepted that his brother was the smart one when they were only tykes, yet he still liked to be the big brother – the one that said what they'd be doing that day, and to lay down the law when necessary. Any jealousy he might have had towards his brother was subdued by a recent revelation unveiled to him – girls were pretty darn pretty. His adolescent affection was directed to one young lady in particular. Pidgie was, to any other observer, an ordinary girl with no outstanding quality. A lovely girl to be sure; well-mannered and intelligent, a real 'girl-next-door'. She'd never be one needing to swat the suitors away with arrogance, but she saw that as beneficial, because looks fade away and smarts bring in the pay. To Balfour she was the one and only; he'd never love another; better to die than to spare her the praise she deserved. As such both boy and girl were left at odds to work out their strange new emotions: Balfour was uncertain how to express his affection aptly while the reserved Pidgie still needed to figure out how to humbly accept being the centre of someone's attention.

It was Rheneas' idea to go see the Wights. The fascination of such a well-known mystery was too much for his young mind to ignore – he simply must see them for himself. The fearful rebuke his parents threw down missed its mark completely and only increased his eagerness.

"Don't go breaking your old lady's heart, boy," his father would say, "trekking through the darkness will bring a world of trouble."

But Balfour had other ideas. Knowing his brother's obsession with spooks and scares he decided that yes, they should try and see the ghosts for themselves, and maybe Pidgie would like to come along too - wouldn't she be impressed? The arrival of a clear day had filled their hearts with anticipation; all through the long school hours they persevered knowing that tonight, tonight they could make their move. So while the merchants packed up their wares and closed up their awnings the boys waited, killing time kicking the football around the oval. It was all too simple really. They'd play rugby until nightfall (as they often did) and claim that they had lost track of time and had to walk Pidgie home. *Heroic! Such good boys*, their parents would say – and nobody's the wiser.

Balfour Woodnote sent the ball flying high with an almighty kick.

The younger boy tore down the field, *Here's Woodnote on the burst!*

The sky had darkened in the last few minutes.

All he has to do is contest the kick and TRRRYYY! The Hammerheads win the championship game; the young fullback Rheneas Woodnote, what a star!

The sky was too dark. Rheneas fumbled the ball. *Well, that's ok, it's not a real game...*

"Can't see nothing anymore," called Balfour.

Rheneas kicked the ball to Pidgie, the oval thing bouncing favourably for her. Balfour looked up, "Moon's in the sky."

"Course," said Rheneas, "where else is it gunna be?"

"Shut up, Rhen."

His brother blushed as Pidgie sniggered softly. *God, he hated his little brother sometimes!* Balfour hoped it was dark enough to shield his red face from Pidgie. Seizing back his hurt authority he stood with arms akimbo and outlined the master plan.

"Right, so we snap a pickie and run. You got the camera, Rhen?"

"Yup!"

"My dad calls 'em the will-of-the-wisp," said Pidgie, "friar's lanterns. Says ghosts aren't for real."

"Maybe so but I reckon everyone at school will be damn stunned to see."

"What if they don't show on the picture?" asked Rheneas.

"You just worry about not dropping that camera; dad'll kill us if you break it. Now, the ghosts might be mad at us disturbing them and all, so we have to be quick. Take the picture and run. I don't plan on being in another story about vanishing!"

"What'll we do if there's trouble?" asked Pidgie.

"There won't be, Pidge," said Balfour proudly, "I'll make sure o' that! Now let's go; it's dark enough!"

Even though he'd thought about this moment for days now, Rheneas suddenly felt the enormous pressure of anticipation; the many nights spent reading his ghost stories, the school days spent daydreaming of an encounter with supernatural had led to this. Maybe his dream was about to become reality; what joy he'd feel witnessing such a rare phenomenon! How crushing the disappointment should his ambition be dashed at the final hurdle! With tensions this high, Rhen tried to prepare himself for potential failure. There was always the possibility that the Wights were mere fable – he had to be ready for that, and although the higher part of his brain braced for it, deep down he knew there'd be no stemming the sting should defeat ensue. But he was a logical boy – where there was a chance, there was hope. The trio slipped through the sandstone streets without drawing much attention to themselves and soon found themselves surrounded by the Norfolk pines. Had their surroundings been dark before, it was pitch black now. The shadows of those giant trees loomed ominously over them, cutting out any light cast by the moon. No sound could crest the distant rush of the sea; waves flung themselves shore-bound with reckless abandon to the beat of footsteps crunching on fallen pine needles. Rheneas could barely remember a time where he'd felt so alive! In spite of the darkness his senses sharpened, the blood pounded in his ears, his nostrils inhaled the scent of feverish sweat. Balfour brought them to a halt at the foot of a natural staircase, and the trio camped themselves in the obstruction of a large sandstone block. If the ghosts had their lanterns, they'd see the children if they were not hidden. The camera shook in Rhen's cold hands.

Why are they so cold?

His armpits were drenched in nervous sweat; he'd taken pictures many times with his dad's antique polaroid, but now he doubted his own ability to hold the thing steady. Nobody was going to believe him with just a blurry photograph as evidence. The sea throbbed noisily in the background; the three behind the rock were silent. How much time had passed? How long would they have to wait? The voice of Balfour echoed in his brother's head – *the Norfolk Wights are always there on clear nights*. It was simply a matter of time.

She would not admit it, but Pidgie felt frightened. Would it be boring to hope nothing showed up? The idea sounded delightful to her at that point; quash the ideas of ghosts and goblins and go home to stuff her face with her mother's home cooking. Then bed, straight to bed – yes that sounded wonderful. The tawny owls cooed, the sea roared and Pidgie hated the deafening silence of nature. Something had to break that chaotic din, and something did. It was subtle at first – a glimpse of teal-coloured light in the gloom that could easily be mistaken for a trick of the eyes. But no, it was there, and look here – there was more than one. Above the rush of waves came a haunting chant of ominous baritone, and one by one the ghosts faded into view – thin green things floating up the natural staircase. A shivering groan escaped from one of the children's' mouths – who it was, none of them would remember later. The gait of the Norfolk Wights was smooth as to give the impression of levitation, indeed no feet could be seen beneath their glowing robes. Pidgie reached for Balfour's hand, but the thing was limp as a dead fish, twice as clammy to the touch, and she saw that the young man was paralysed with fear and had ceased to notice the presence of her or his brother. Pidgie whimpered softly and nudged Rheneas, "Do it, then! Take the photo!"

Shocked back into action Rheneas fumbled the big camera, and if not for the strap about his shoulder it would have fallen onto the rock. He took one frantic second to adjust the focus and – flash! The camera let out a mighty bright light that lit up the forest for the briefest moment. The camera groaned as it processed itself and when their eyes had readjusted the three kids felt their stomachs drop all at once. The Wights, interrupted of their ritual, had all turned to face the disturbance, and Rheneas could only cry in horror at the sight of their skinless faces and sardonic grins. The eyes – awful red things – all pierced the resilience of the young intruders with a glare of mindless hatred. *What are you doing here?* – those eyes implied. Rheneas had heard of 'fight or flight' and it seemed his body would do neither, until he was yanked away by Pidgie and Balfour and all three broke into a feverish dash.

"Run!" cried Balfour, trailing the other two.

Behind them they heard a sickening shriek; Rhen took half a second to glance over his shoulder and saw the banshees had given chase. He could not see a thing in the darkness, but that didn't matter – they had to get away from there. All around the teal lights flickered about, illuminating the tree trunks and throwing shadows on the rocky ground beneath them.

"Here!" yelled Rheneas.

With a thud they fell into the shelter of a small alcove, and Rheneas blacked out.

When he awoke, the morning breeze fluttered against his face, and the rarity of another day of sunshine greeted him. The camera was in pieces – Rheneas must have fallen on it when he dove into the shallow cave. He sat up and felt pain race through his thigh; yep, he'd fallen on the camera. He heard a quivering breath next to him – it was Pidgie, and as they looked at one another with surprise they realised two things. The sun had shown its face for the second day running, and Balfour was missing.

Captain Ivy Festoon

Most folk across the Continent knew of its upper western shoreline despite the fact that very few lived there. What made it so infamous was the inhospitable conditions that seemed to actively despise humanity, and wish to keep it away at any cost. Truly its craggy shoals were suited only to the sea birds; even the fat sea lions that resided on the rocks would shift with discomfort as the rough and salt-bitten cliffs dug into their fleshy skin. In times past the place had been called Towers Rocks, although as to why had been lost to the ages. To everyone else on the Continent, it was called the Bleak Coast. It was a frontline for the ever-waging battle betwixt land and ocean – Behemoth versus Leviathan – and pride alone appeared to be the reason neither side was willing to yield an inch of the unenviable territory. Yes, the sea spray lashed against the cliff faces, rusting away the coast by the millimetre, while the iron-grey mountains thrust their stalagmites through the pained surface of the awful green sea. Cheer was an unknown quality to the Bleak Coast, and its less than favourable currents and weather meant that most ship traffic avoided it at all costs.

Centuries ago, the Vikings had been able to taunt the wild winds to their advantage; their epic sails catching hold of the gale and sending their vessels on a risky beeline to the sunnier south, but in the age of steam the newer fishing boats had no such need or desire. Most deemed life too valuable to risk for the malnourished fish that circled in the waters; even the birds knew their harvest was stunted, and a terrible vestigial instinct kept them from flying to a brighter haven. As such it was unusual to say that the horizon disclosed a blemish in the shape of a small tug on one stark morning (a spring day in name only), and this tug spun its big rear wheel through the swell as its crew tried to ignore the uncomfortable rain that fell. Captain Ivy Festoon, the youngest woman to ever pilot these waters, could not see the shoreline from her vantage point at the bridge. Be it fog or miles that hid land from view, Ivy did not care, for it was something quite different that she and her crew searched for.

Eyes forward always, that's what her papa had taught her, *the sea is a fickle beast that demands respect and gives none in return.*

The temptation to scour the surface for that which she desired was strong, but she had to trust her crew. Ah, but the eyes of her first mate grew weaker by the day – Old Mate Valentine they called him, and Squabble was young; green around the gills, a greenhorn – even his wool pullover was green; could Ivy trust those two in the crow's nest? Better them than Brine, the burly workhorse of a sailor whose sole talent was shovelling coal into the ship's gullet. Ivy had to work with what she had, and everyone had told her that her distrustful nature was a flaw she would spend a lifetime remedying. Her craft, the *Poison Ivy*, was a sturdy old thing christened thusly by her father who had clearly displayed a fascination towards the sinuous plant. The boat had been in Ivy's life as long as she'd known which led her to believe that it was she who took after the boat's namesake.

How terribly belittling, she'd often thought, although she could never doubt the adoration her father lavished on her, his only kin. To think of him was to cut her heart, even though a decade had passed since he had left the world. The sea always reminded her of him, but now was not the time to be maudlin; things changed quickly in those waters and only the wary made it through. Deep was hardly the word to describe the seas off the Bleak Coast, for in its shallow wake lurked many a reef and rock that could gut a ship like a fish and doom its crew to its watery graveyard. Stories of the mirage island travelled all up and down the western coasts, and the shanties only speculated on what wonderful things were stored inside its subterranean labyrinths. So fanciful were stories of a long-lost treasure island that few believed the tales, and so treacherous the region that no sailors were foolhardy enough to seek it. Nobody that is, save for young miss Ivy Festoon who, with little aplomb or fanfare had steered her crew to what she called the ultimate pay day – yes, she was sure of this one.

"Whirlpool," called Squabble from the crow's nest.

"Aye," Ivy replied, almost mechanically and spun the wheel starboard; the ocean was littered with them here – maelstroms small and large – all of them dangerous.

Old Mate Valentine, whose shoulders doubled Ivy's svelte width, lumbered into the bridge with a weathered map.

"We here, Captain," he said, "least the map say so."

"You may be right, Old Val," Ivy smirked.

Valentine slipped his hand under his wool cap and scratched his bald head. With his other hand he tugged at a little bell pull next to the wheel, and a solemn echo rang down below deck.

"Hold there, Briney!"

Usually, Brine could not hear his captain's feminine voice from above him, but with Valentine's thunderous baritone there was no denying – he snuffed out the coal fire and the ship began to slow.

Step, step, thud! "Ow!"

"Use the ladder, Squabble," Ivy sighed with a shake of the head.

Bedraggled and sniffling, the young ship picked himself up from the foot of the lookout he'd attempted to jump off. Squab's antics amazed his captain – *she'd* certainly never been quite so *dumb* at his age. He too, stepped into the bridge and tousled his bird-mad hair.

How was it that someone so ingrained in the sailor life be so pasty and twitchy? Never mind.

Squabble had no idea of Ivy's internal judgement and smiled cheerfully, "Think this is it? Not much of an island."

"*Desolation's Shore* – yes, maybe," replied Ivy.

"The old poem had me thinking it'd be bigger," mumbled Valentine.

Indeed, there was no much to be looked at. Breaking the surface ever so slightly, so desperately, there stood the impression of a rocky outcrop unique to any other they'd seen. Hardly an impressive expanse – only a few yards either way – yet from its centre loomed a small alcove, a hood-like rock that seemed to open into a shale decline towards a cavern. Nothing else was given away by its sepulchral stature, just a shuddering aura of anticipation electrocuting Captain Ivy Festoon. She felt it; this must be the place. Brine, face dirtied with labour, had emerged behind them and shivered like a simpleton.

"Das a bad place, Captain; ain't making me go down that cave, no please."

Ivy tied back her auburn hair and stood facing her crew, arms akimbo. Even though both Valentine and Brine were at least a decade older than her they still looked to her as a motherly figure, and there was no denying the tender intellect she employed to her beloved crew mates. Often, they trusted her without question; today she saw no such confidence. Squabble hid his eyes beneath messy black curls; Valentine had scratched his head so much that it had a slight bleed; Brine stood hunched so that even his hulking frame looked miniscule. Ivy's thoughts raced; she had to work quickly to retain her trust – a good captain would make sure of her crew's wellbeing.

"Gents, I don't know what's inside that cavern. Hell, tides might mean we only have a few hours to explore but we've traversed more perilous oceans than any silly cave could throw at us!"

"Tisn't the dark, captain," said Brine, "is a bad vibe I has. Ghosts o' the past and such."

"I think Briney is onto something, captain," piped Valentine, "if this *is* the Desolation Shore, hadn't we best let sleeping dogs lie? Don't wanna go disrespecting no old laws."

"Please guys, do you *see* any ghosts? Any person? Any bird, fish or sea lion?! If there *was* anything in there to hurt us, it would be long gone. Nobody comes through these waters."

"The tide?" said Squabble.

"Does the same thing each day," replied Ivy, "In, out, up down. We can time our exploration and be back on board for tea. Brine, how much coal we got?"

"Enough,"

"Good, then we bring a sack and leave a trail so we don't get lost – I don't know how deep that cavern is. Still got plenty of oil for lanterns too. So, what say you lot?"

The trio looked to the floor, kicked at the boards and shrugged their shoulders. Captain Festoon had never led them astray before; surely they could trust her to guide them through a cave, especially given the rough seas she'd so aptly navigated before.

Brine manned the oars, Valentine and Squabble kept a keen eye on the surface to ensure their little boat didn't snag. Somehow maintaining her balance Ivy stood and surveyed the little island, every now and then turning her eye back to the anchored steamboat as it bobbed this way and that like a kite. The tide was receding – they'd have a solid few hours, and she hoped that there would be enough to justify the expedition. She would hate to peer into the cave mouth and realise it only went down a few metres. No, that wouldn't happen; that intuition burned so hotly in her gut, telling her that there was something here. And when the quartet stood at the gaping entrance and felt a sickly air resonate from within, she knew her predictions were accurate. For that breeze – frigid and loveless – could only issue forth from the absolute depths of earth where time was swallowed. Wordless they gathered, readied the lanterns despite the moist air subduing their flames to tepid whispers.

"Follow my lead," said Ivy before she was stopped by Brine's hairy forearm.

"No cap, allow me. We can't have you being injured."

"This be true," added Old Valentine, "and I'll flank your other side. Squabby can bring up the rear and lay the coal trail."

Those first timid steps into the cave mouth were difficult even for the adventurous young captain. In there the sea roared, its bellows echoing off of the wet walls and encompassing the intruders, as if to give them one last warning – *get out*. The floor was ashen and littered with a slippery slate; the little rocks were moss-eaten and loose, giving way under the softest footfalls, so Brine went perilously close to losing his footing on several occasions. Chained by held hands the four of them felt each bump and slide; were one to lose balance the rest would do well to keep their own. Ivy Festoon considered the two hands she held – Brine's almost simian appendage and Valentine's ancient and spidery digits. Behind her came the reverberated click-click-click of Squabble dropping a piece of coal every few paces. It would be tough to differentiate the coal from the cave's native rocks – this Ivy knew – but so long as the lanterns held out she'd be able to locate those stones with no reflection, as everything within the cave glistened with moisture. Already the light of the entrance had vanished and she believed them to have descended some fifty feet below. It was better than she had thought; this must have been some forgotten air pocket where the ocean had not penetrated. As the cave deepened so too did her child-like fascination and expectations for what they might find.

"So dark..." Brine whimpered; Ivy could hear the fear in his voice.

"You've a little light and plenty of company," she whispered reassuringly.

Even their whispers carried far, and Ivy begun to think they might have left the tunnels and entered some large and echoing void. The echoes, stitched as they were with shadow, seemed to expand and contract with the diminished din of the ocean above them; just as time was apparently forgotten in this extreme depth, so too was the concept of space. Had they ventured miles or metres? Seconds or hours? It was enough to make Ivy swoon – surely the human mind could not comprehend the vastness of this underworld. On, on they went, always slowly but with increasing confidence, while click-click-click went Squabble behind them. Ivy dared not leave the safety of the group, but on a sudden became aware of an ethereal glow in the pitch black. Like distant galaxies an aching blue blurred dimly in places; Ivy thought herself to be hallucinating as she pondered the eerie glow. Images of deep-sea fish with little lights dangling over their heads filled her mind and when Squabble noted the blue glow as well she knew it was no apparition.

"The stones," whispered Valentine.

"Eh?" muttered Brine.

"The stones are glowing."

Pertaining to the glut of darkness and her crippled senses, Ivy felt dizzy. The blue glow was not strong enough to illuminate the cavern, and she almost wished it would go away. It confused her; went against all the natures of logic she knew – how could a light exist yet reflect off of nothing? Ivy's ears piqued to every small noise that sounded, compensating for her diminished vision – the roaring sea, the dripping cavern, the clack of rocks and – *the faint sound of laughter*. Surely, she had imagined it. Robbed of natural function her brain had to have been playing tricks on her. Yet there it was – laughter that sounded again, too distant and childish to belong to her crew mates; it was a timorous and stifled giggle, like that of a child hiding while her friend sought. Fear began to creep into her heart as she considered her friends; the fact that they had not reacted to the laughter frightened her. Yet she was too afraid to inquire; were the laughter fictitious she feared madness, but to confirm the its reality was a whole new thing all together.

There was a splash, close and loud, that rocked Ivy to her senses, and the jolt in her hand told her that Brine had stepped into water. The water was like ice, and Brine leapt back and brought the party to a halt. As their lamp shone over the surface of water before them, they could discern that the cave tunnel continued onward – albeit submerged. They had reached a dead-end.

"Can't go no further," said Brine.

"Timely," replied Squab, "coal's running low."

Ivy Festoon cursed through her teeth. The cave went on further! That it was blocked off to her by something as simple as water pushed her frustration to a head. There had to be a way to continue! She snatched the lantern off of Brine and surveyed the area. With its light only going so far, she could not tell how long that underwater tunnel was; it could be ten metres or ten miles, and that mystery irritated her greatly. The risk could not be justified – to paddle through the blackness only to run out of air, and to reach desperately for the surface only to be met by the touch of the submerged cave roof – Ivy shuddered to think of it.

"Don't think these lamps will last much longer either, captain," said Valentine, "and the tide's only going to rise from here. We have to turn back."

"Argh! No!" hissed Ivy, "There's more to this cavern! Just look at those stones! Have you ever seen a rock glow like that?"

"I think you're right, Miss Festoon. We've stumbled on something special here, but you have to admit its secrets won't be revealed to us today." Valentine said.

The old mate was showing his age now; he'd walked the earth longer than his captain, and felt deserving of a certain respect from his junior at that moment. There was also the hint of fear in his voice – only a slight quaver, yet he hoped his young captain wouldn't notice that and instead take heed to his aged wisdom.

"Scared." Brine whimpered pathetically.

Squabble tossed his head to and fro, fearing the tide might overtake them at any moment. It could not be denied that panic had crept into the mood and was spreading to each of them. The water had risen – only slightly, but the splash of it against Squabble's ankle sent him into a frenzy. He scrambled back up the shale slide with one of the two lanterns dwindling around his belt.

"Squab, no!" cried Valentine.

It was too late; the young ship-hand slipped, and with a bloodcurdling shatter the lamp was snuffed out. In the chaos Old Mate Valentine snatched his captain's wrist and begged her to relinquish the other lantern. His eyes glistened with desperation in the darkness. Yet Ivy would not be moved.

"Please captain," said Val, "the lantern!"

They fought for their remaining light and Ivy cried, "No! Not now, not when we're so close! Get a hold of yourself!"

The confliction of a sense of adventure and of claustrophobia mounted in her breast and outpoured in a savage backhand to Valentine's face. The force of her swat surprised them both; it was clear however that Captain Ivy Festoon was possessed by a flurry of madness. In their struggles the oil lantern flew from their grasp and all at once, before any of them could react, the lamp fell into the water at their feet and was extinguished. The dark was instant and impenetrable, and Brine could be heard adding his own scream to Squabble's frightened wail. Ivy realised then that they had made a fatal error, that they were now trapped underground with no light and a rising tide. Although her eyes were devoid of sight altogether, her ears pained with the violence of noise surrounding – her crew mate's screams, the roar of the ocean, and *again* that sinister laughter. Her father's words returned to her once more – *what would a good captain do at this time?* Fighting her own fears, she cried out to her crew and implored them to remain calm; she would get them out of this. However, Brine and Squabble would not stop screaming, and Ivy was overwhelmed with such sound as to make her go deaf.

"Your hands! Give me your hands! We get out together!"

She continued her vain attempt to regain order, her own shouting becoming more desperate; until she suddenly stopped and listened. The wailing had stopped; all that remained was the rush of the ocean above them. Even the laughter had ceased, but instead of calm the silence instead brought more fear – Ivy Festoon felt absolutely and impossibly alone.

"Val?" she whimpered, "Brine? Squab?"

No answer.

"Anybody? Please... Give me your hand."

Ivy groped at the darkness, and for but a moment she felt a rush of relief as she clasped at another hand. That hope would be horribly brief – for she realised that the hand that grasped her was not one of her crewmates, no. *It was undoubtedly the hand of a child.* The laughter sounded again, closer, and a fresh scream burst from Ivy's mouth.

Of Frost-Bitten Fields

In the Mid-North the earth was dead, and all that lay root there was known to adorn itself with the same cadaverous quality. As the seeds of Spring floated along on their annual sojourn they'd shiver to drift over those highlands, knowing that to land there was to struggle against a shallow and poisonous soil, to be choked by the thorns. Just as one might avoid a particular neighbourhood, knowing too well that to traverse that path was a *danse macabre,* your wary companions might say with infectious nausea, 'let us go this other way instead.' Pity be the vagabond who wandered across those frost-bitten fields, where the down-and-out would drown in stagnant sorrow. Still, those less fortunate would find themselves under the iron-grey skies not by their own design; there were the poor children (many of whom had not been children for many a year) whose guardian stars played a divine prank on them and saw them born in that savage land.

The people that grew there were not unlike the plants that could survive there; crude, harsh, uncompromising and, perhaps most unfortunately, accepting of their fate. Their settlements dotted the ochre countryside with awkward stature; shanty towns bent and twisted with corpuscles of corrugated iron and canvas. Carnivalesque, bizarre – even here in this forgotten place they looked as if they did not belong, that maybe they were just passing through. Maybe by tomorrow they'd disassemble themselves; but unlike a travelling circus these freaks had nowhere to be, and nobody expected them anywhere else. They might adorn themselves with streamers of faded colour flags, or hang the skins of their hunt on the gnarled claws of the dead trees, but there was no hiding the fact – they were death dressed up as life.

Iggy Oberon of the frost-bitten fields slammed his shovel into the soil and stretched his spidery arms. There was no use in continuing his trade; the sun was about an hour away and once the daylight hit the fields it was better to be in the shade. He shoved a cigarette into his teeth and cursed at this land of extremes, of which there was no in-between. By night the frost strangled the breath of those sickly people, finding any bare flesh to harass with its unwelcome touch and filling one's lungs with a pneumonic residue. And by day, the heat of the sun would sear the soil, bake in the oppression and wring out what little moisture it could. Iggy watched as his shovel fell over. If there was water to be found here, he'd have smelled it. But Coldchop had been certain; that stupid stick of his had wavered frantically at this special spot of soil, and Lord knew his back wasn't up to the task of unearthing the precious resource.

"Look at that fool," Iggy sighed, "If he be so sure o' the water under this here ground then why's he still doing that bloody rain dance?"

He became aware of the rhythmic crush of the other shovel cutting the earth; whether Thorn-Petal realised it or not, her shovel-falls fell in unison with Coldchop's distant dancing.

"Why'd ye think I keep on working so?" she snapped, "Keep yerself busy and ye won't have to notice him t'all."

"Well," said Iggy, "y'all campaigned to get all the work."

Thorn-Petal stopped and glared at him, "Said we wanted equal rights, ye shiftless spit-flapper."

"I hear, I hear; come Thornie, ye know I jest. Not like there's coin to share around here anyways."

Iggy scratched at his sandy hair and chuckled. He was an ugly man, but his joviality was infectious.

Thorn-Petal fashioned a smile, if only to shut him up, and shifted her big body around to an untapped patch of soil. She dug deep, Iggy smoked, Coldchop danced; not much else happened for what seemed a long while. This trance was ended by a different kind of shovel sound – a cymbal crash at the end of a phrase; Thorn-Petal's trowel struck something other than dirt. She readjusted her thick black hair before retrieving the foreign object: a rusted automaton toy that had somehow found itself decaying out there in the Mid-North. Thorn-Petal brushed the sediment off the soup can man and smiled.

"No water, but another one them little metal men."

"Kids'll be happy."

"Yer, still thirsty too."

"Always a barrel of optimism, Thornie. Here, let old uncle Iggy give 'em it."

"Dream on, creep. Kids hate me enough for making 'em eat their root veggies – I'll take whatever I can get."

"But they's getting sick of me only finding copper wires; imagination only goes so far playin' with wire."

Thorn-Petal smirked, "Better get back to diggin' then boy-o!"

The sky grew a lighter shade of grey, but no sun had crept out just yet. Maybe the day would be overcast. A reprieve, perhaps? Not for Iggy Oberon; if the weather allowed it, it'd see him stuck out there digging all day.

Will still need the ol' cork hat but, thought Iggy, *Sun might take the day off, but the blow-flies won't.*

The insects might be bothersome to him, but Iggy Oberon loved the swarms of children that would gather round him from across the shanty town. They loved old uncle Iggy, begged him for stories, for treasures he'd found in the fields and Iggy, gathering little respect from his peers, adored the idolatry the chillun would lavish on him. Deep down he realised it was because they knew no better. Leave the discipline to others more responsible; was no way he'd be a downer. Life was tough enough for these kids already. Thorn-Petal was right; he'd better get back to digging. The wind picked up, mercifully stirring the highlands from their stagnation. Wind chimes sounded sweetly, and Iggy heard Coldchop grunt as his dance increased in tempo.

"It's working!" cried Coldchop.

Thorn-Petal shook her head sadly and muttered, "No. No it's not…"

"Hoo ha!" Coldchop thrust his stick skyward.

But just like that the wind stopped and the chimes slowed to a still. Iggy crushed his cigarette and turned to Thorn-Petal, "Well? Anything?"

"Just mud. Not enough to drink."

In the distance Coldchop cried with anguish, "No! No, no, no!"

He threw his stick to the ground, his many bracelets tinkling, and almost tripped over his poncho, so oversized was it on his stumpy frame.

"Next time, Chops!" called Iggy.

"I was so close this time."

"Goin' home," said Thorn-Petal, "ain't wasting no more strength. Git yer shovel, Ig."

"Yeah darlin'."

He grabbed both shovels and the three of them wandered back along the main boulevard of the shanty town. Creatures lurked about the dusty thoroughfare, sharing the path with the humans who towered over them. A few chickens pecked about skittishly, while the frilled-necked lizards yelled their gruff guttural utterances. A couple of skinny brumbies brayed in the fields, picking what grass they could from around the barbed wire fence posts. Iggy Oberon slumped into his makeshift couch and threw his cork hat over his face. His was a crude abode, even amongst those dirty dwellings. He had little to call his own, but his old couch and his guitar were all he felt necessary to claim. The guitar had been out of service for some time now; the copper wires made a decent substitute for the odd snapped string but nothing sounded quite like steel, and steel was rare. Across the way Thorn-Petal and Coldchop conversed while a few children jumped around Thornie's hips begging for candy. They took greedily, stuffed pieces in their mouths; none of them knew when they'd eat again. Having gotten that which they were after they raced over to Iggy with sugar-stained smiles.

"Uncle Iggy! Mutt says you outran a shark once!"

"Shut it, Churl; I did not! Sharks are in the water anyhow."

Mutt pouted from under his bowl cut and yanked at one of Churl's pigtails, causing her to squeal like the namesake of her dirty hair. Churl punched him back for good measure.

"Well nah, kiddies," Iggy replied, "but old mayor Coldchop once boxed a Drowsy-Bear; wore a pair of echidnas for gloves, I remember."

"That was brother Foldclop!" cried Coldchop.

"Tryin' talk you up, chief," Iggy sighed.

An emaciated woman yelled from her tent, "Quit filling their heads with fables, Ig."

"I don't tell no fables, Rosie," he tapped his noggin', "Why all my adventures are locked in here. Just giving you kids a hope of leaving this place one day."

"Now you're being silly." said Thorn-Petal.

"Yes," added Coldchop, "the drought will break! My dance came so close!"

Mutt and Churl sat before Iggy; a few other kids soon joined.

"Don't die wondering, kids. Die wandering! Pity be a man who accepts one place; the world goes far beyond the Mid-North."

Mutt gasped, "You mean… Mid-South?"

Churl punched him again, "No dummy! Next-To-North! Or Behind-Us-North, right Uncle Iggy?"

"North-South-Nowhere, kiddies! Left-Right-Down-And-Out! But you'll never know if you just listen to old fart Coldchop!"

The kids giggled and Coldchop pouted.

"Why," Iggy continued, "My mother had a brother, whose sister had a mister, whose uncle, who'da thunk'll leave you quaking in your boots. For those who never go are sure to aptly throw their life to the dogs and live in deathly frightening fog."

Iggy basked in the glow of bulbous eyes that were ripe with anticipation. It was story time, the children knew it, and with Uncle Iggy's snippet of eloquence (which seemingly only appeared when telling a tale, and would vanish soon after) they were hooked.

"Now I heard this from a friend, who heard it from a foe, about a friend whose other friend had inner demons as his foe…"

And Iggy Oberon began his story.

Mortal Curse

For this friend o' mine, to write a will was a strange thing. It inherently acknowledged his mortality; a signing off one's allotted portion of time. Kiddies, life can be dark when you consider it, flanked at either end by black curtains - at birth and death - and one can do no more than stagger forward blindly with a candle flame that illuminates only as far as the old faith commands. My friend who wrote this will - perhaps he'd turned to thinking perhaps a little too deeply on things. He had a friend who had recently died. Now this man wanted no consolations, for he fell from communication with this fellow many years earlier, and he had died at an admirable age – probably a number bigger than your uncle Ig can count to! Here's what he told me.... *(Here Iggy Oberon procured a wad of papers – letters, it would seem, from this so-called friend of his, although whether he knew the author or merely wished to claim the accolades of a good story, one could not know for certain).*

'I know all too well the pangs of grief, having lost - like many - peoples of whom my life has been so deeply rooted. No, I feel I won't cry for the man, at least I haven't before, but there was a peculiar circumstance surrounding his demise; something that tickled a rather macabre fancy in my oft drifting mind; a sort of sinister darkness of memories I haven't not recalled since my youth. At my age the mind starts to play tricks; happenings that once seemed so real, I must now remind myself of their truth, whilst reminding myself that other monsters are just dreams. But no, the events of this tale are true - of that I pledge with utmost surety.

'A little about this friend - a hard man, not unkind, but deeply serious and (I believed) unshakeably confident in himself and his views. He was a staunch atheist. The very mention of God, or rather anything incomprehensible by the human eye made him laugh and taunt of faeries and Father Christmas. Why do I raise this quality, you may ask? For in spite of his resolute stance, I have reason to suggest his later years greatly compromised this; inasmuch as my last visit with him presented him almost unrecognisable to the proud young man who had been my friend. I find it remarkable that one man may dismiss what another assuredly claims as truth, and alas I may appear as such to any who listen to this here tale.

'There is no defence for the troubled soul, as you, reader, shall soon hear; for what use are your battlements when the enemy has already entered your home, invited by dread, furnished by fear?

'My home town lay within a bleak countryside' – *no! Not Mid-North, kids. Another squalor, where them snootier folk might chuckle at the furnishings; at the daemon-fearing citizens, at the garlic wreaths hung in ramshackle kitchens, of beads and crucifixes and other idols clutched fearfully to sallow chests!*

'We lived simple lives; my friends and I traipsing the muddy fields with our crudely made football after long hours of assisting our fathers in their farm work. My mother was a suspicious one; blessing our souls at the sound of sneezes, calling for the devil to take us when we misbehaved. Even then the friend of whom I speak - his name being Ashen - had no issue in 'correcting' my mother,

'"Ain't no such thing as curses and angels, ma'am," he'd say.

'An admirable woman, my mother felt no need to argue with a child, choosing to shoo us away from her sight lest we "wished for a red back porch!"

'By the time we were teens Ashen would have said that he knew the world - nothing could stand in the way of his claimed wisdom - a trait that the young girls of the village swooned over. It would appear that my friend would have little issues in life, as a likeable man of full confidence he always seemed a winner in the eyes of the townsfolk.

'"You lack ambition," relatives would say of me, *and who here would say that about old Iggy today?* "mayhaps you should strive to be more like Ashen. Now there's a lad who'll no doubt move to things greater than this dismal town!"

'"Pride cometh before a fall," an adage my old man often quoted.

'I say our town had little fanfare, as such you could imagine the excitement conjured by the travelling gypsy circus that visited late one summer. For those that remained in the village year-round, it stood as one moment when they could converse with the outside world and shudder with fear of the unknown. They arrived in caravans and pitched their tents in the fields, and for but a brief moment a splash of colour overlaid itself on the rain-soaked terrain. Along with the coloured canvas and lights and flags came the din. A cheerful din to be sure; the sounds of laughter and bustle were enough to warm the iciest heart.

'Our mothers would not see us for days at a time, so much did my friends and I peruse that carnival. My father was less than impressed - he was one to view such a festival as a waste of time. A waste of time may have been the wrong choice of words considering; but for my friend Ashen, a shadow was undoubtedly cast over his remaining decades. One tent, cruder than most, slouched inconspicuously betwixt other, grander displays, where within dwelt a haggard gypsy, would stand as a threshold to death for Ashen.

Now don't look so scared, kids.

'The so-called clairvoyant, who called to us from the crowd, immediately impressed a foreboding dread on me heart.

'"A fortune for the young lads, perhaps?" she croaked, to which the two of us merely shrugged; having grown somewhat weary of the other attractions, we were happy to oblige. Upon entering the tent, it would take a moment for our eyes to adjust to the dim lighting, and the cloying smell of incense hung heavily in the air. Ensconced at a small table she beckoned us to sit, when my friend hesitated sluggishly.

'"This is foolishness," said he, "there is nothing of interest here. Come, friend."

'Here the lady laughed, and there was something in that guffaw that sent shivers down my spine, "Will not the young man give an old woman the time of day? I can assure you will leave a wiser man!"

'"Hag!" retorted my friend, "You can offer nothing."

'"Come now, Ashen. I will impart knowledge of your future! Allow me to unveil what is yet to pass!"

'Here my friend seized up, "How came you to know my name? Speak, woman!"

'Again, the woman laughed, "I know more of you than you know yourself! For I can read the mind, read the heart, see the future."

"'None can claim this." says Ashen.

"'And yet I knew your name," said the old hag, "and know that you are a sceptical man - what you progressive types coin as an atheist."

'I had meanwhile sat quietly and listened to this exchange, feeling at this moment the need to mediate the situation, although had I my time over, I would have joined my friend in egressing.

'Instead, I spoke, "Let us humour her, Ashen. What harm?"

"'Principle!" he spat, though appeared to calm after this, "I suppose it is only fair that the worldlier have ears for the simple."

'He sat. The clairvoyant paid no heed to the backhanded insult served by Ashen, and still that sickly smile remained on her wrinkled face.

"'Youths," she would smirk, "always so dismissive. The world is far older than you or I. Its mysteries remain unearthed; you two need proof of my legitimacy? You, young man. Your mother is named Lizabeth."

'Here she pointed at me. My heart at once fell to the pit of my stomach. How in the world did she know my mother's name?

"'Your expression says enough," whispered the old hag, she turned to Ashen, "and you. Your family hails from Elgin."

"'A lucky guess," replied Ashen, "deduced from my accent. Nothing more."

"'You are a stony-hearted one. Hear this then, a scar runs along your right ankle - the remnants of an injury attained while running through the woods as a child. You tripped against a rotten log."

'This seemed to be enough to reluctantly convince Ashen. Still he gazed suspiciously at the woman, no doubt plagued with similar questions to my own. How did she know such things? What possible explanation could be applied that did not involve witchcraft or other-worldly mania?

"'Allow me this - I will tell you of your final words! I can reveal the very last thing you will utter before death! Will you hear it?" she inquired.

"'Again, I must scoff," interjected Ashen, "and say that none can know that."

"'He believes for but a second, then slips back into ignorance. Stubborn boy."

"'Fine," he huffed, "tell me then. Do you need my palm? Perhaps a rosary? Some magic dust? Shall I chant for you?"

'Incensed at this taunt, the old hag grasped at his wrists most violently and closed her eyes tightly. It would look almost as if she were in the throes of death, so intense were those contorted grimaces, before she opened her eyes. I immediately saw the look of melancholy in her composure. She shook her head sadly, much to the frustration of Ashen, whose patience was clearly dwindled.

"'Out with it then, witch!" he said.

'But the woman hesitated; the change that had come over her was unsettling, "Are you sure you would like to hear?"

'Ashen was unmoved, "Humour me."

'She sighed, "Your final words, those words which will carry you into the grave are thus - Somebody help me."

'For a moment silence crept into the tent; all that could be heard was the chatter of peoples in the carnival outside. My friend furrowed his brow; immediately I had thought his reaction would be one of retort, and why not? He had made his disdain to the black arts vehement. Instead, he appeared fraught with worry, as though the very sentence that would prelude his doom croaked at the back of his throat.

'"My last words are that of distress?" he muttered finally.

'The old hag tutted sadly, "I wish I could have told you otherwise, but have I not been correct in all other facets during this little discourse? I am never wrong, boy."

'"A colourful joke," said I in a vain attempt to dispel the tension, "perhaps we should leave, Ashen."

'"N-no matter," replied Ashen, although he clearly wasn't listening to me, "I will simply alter that course. If I never utter those words, I suppose I shall alter my fate!"

'The hag shook her head, "Fate is not something that can be altered, young man. Though there may be twists in the tail, the end is reached all the same."

'"Come now, Ashen," said I, "let us leave."

'And I practically had to drag the man out of the tent.

'The months would pass in that same lethargic manner native to our hometown. The carnival left soon after; the cavalry of caravans rattling off down the north road and out of sight until the next year when, as though it had lapped the world in twelve months, it would appear again, this time arriving from the south. The alterations of Ashen's persona were immediate and macabre. Even with my reminders of his usual stoicism, the hammer blow of the hag's frightful words had left their shattered mark, and nothing seemed to lever him from the pessimism and indeed, paranoia, that within he had become undoubtedly wedged. It pained me to see my good friend distressed so, yet I could offer little comfort to soothe his soul. What comfort can the good Lord offer the man who will not turn to see him? Such was the situation when I tried to console. I had little choice but to assume his stance and remind him that clairvoyance is oft trivial, and why should he take such heed of what one senile old woman told him.

'"You don't see my friend," he would reply, "perhaps it isn't her words, but rather finality of what they imply! Say that she is indeed correct: will nothing change the course? If one is doomed to die horribly, can anything I do change it?"

'I shook my head; such things baffled me, and I wondered whether I was not interrogating hard enough, or whether he was overthinking things.

'"Had I have seen her the day preceding, or the day following, would that have changed my final words?" he continued, "Furthermore, can I achieve anything with this knowledge?"

'"Then mayhaps you should see her again? See if the knowledge of those words has led to an alteration of said fate?"

'Here my friend broke into sobs. I stood stunned; never before had I seen him in such distress.

'"Pray tell, Ashen," said I, "why does this obsess you so? Surely one as headstrong as you can ignore this! Who can know for sure of what the future holds? Not I, not you, sir!"

'"I tried to track her down; alas, she is gone! Disappeared! None could vouch for her very existence! I am doomed with this unfinished tale; I am left with only half the information."

'"As you were before!" I replied, "I have just told you, my friend, that none know of what lies ahead!"

'"No. No, no. I know of one thing - that of my life ending in troubled circumstance. And I will change it."

'He paced before me - as I ran my eyes over his dwelling I took notice of the many tomes piled by his writing desk, stitched with titles regarding psychics, premonition, *fate*.

'I would try again to soothe his spirit, "Whether 'destiny' is something pre-assigned matters not. We live in a world filled with risk! Hazards are everywhere, man. I say this not to trouble you; this is part of life and we live accordingly!"

"'Destiny, yes. How can I know if it has changed? How will I know if my end has altered?" he was clearly not listening to me.

'Nothing seemed to sway him from his path; he was utterly convinced of his grisly end.

'When years had passed the day arrived when I would leave the village. Acquiring for myself a profitable career, one which required my presence in the bustle of the city, I would say farewell to the snow globe existence I had kept for so long. My horizons expanded, and rather than stand daunted by their extents I would set out in one direction - the direction I deemed to shine the brightest. It would pain me to leave my old mother, who despite the slow deterioration of her psyche seemed to totter along at a steady pace, defying doctors who would tell her to slow down and rest more. I promised her and father that I would return one day, to which they would reply simply that they hoped (for my own sake, I assure you) my leaving would be permanent.

'By this stage my relationship with Ashen had grown distant. Not so much strained, but we had drifted, anchorless, as childhood friends often do, into waters uncharted by the other. Nonetheless I saw it fit to bid him farewell, to wish him the best in what I assumed would be a bright life for him as well. When I made this final visit, he would appear in the very spot I had last seen him - alone in his quarters. But while the general clutter of furniture and ornament had remained unchanged, Ashen himself had grown emaciated and withered. Perhaps a case of jaundice, he bore the appearance of a tree branch shrivelled with an autumn wind, his hair and skin looking far greyer than the colourful pallor I had known him for. He would, however, be delighted to see me and took little notice of my initial shock at his appearance.

"'You are leaving us!" he croaked cheerfully.

'His mouth smiled, but the eyes were sunken and hollow, clouded with fear and turmoil.

"'Indeed, my good friend," I replied, "and here I was resolutely assured that you would have beaten me to the punch long ago."

'He stood and crept to his solitary window, and I saw furthermore the malnourishment of his figure; his legs cracked at bulbous knees, slippered feet struggled to support his diminished frame.

"'Alas, yes. I had dreams such as yours once - this I know."

"'You must promise, sir, that you will pursue your passions as I know you can."

'Here his eyes quivered, and I fancied he might shed a tear, "Best of luck to you, my dear friend. I cannot leave. The risks I would face, with the fate I am assigned - I won't dare leave yet."

'I furrowed my brow, "Surely you are not still hung up on that silly premonition? It was a passing comment with little foundation."

"'We as men are too fragile," he said, "this body - mortal flesh, is too easily scarred. I am better to stay where I can avoid danger - be that hag correct or no."

'I felt instantly drained and exhausted. I knew there would be little point arguing with the man; even in his feeble state he was still as stubborn as I had ever known him to be.

"'It is good to see you," he said eventually, "I will miss you, my friend."

'We embraced for a final time, and I would cringe at the touch of his hunching back, the bones of his ribs and spine easily felt beneath paper-thin skin.

"'You must promise me that you will not live out your life in fear," I said firmly, "Leave this place when you are ready. The world will be richer for your investment of character."

'He stared through me with a melancholy smile, "I... I will, good friend."

'His response had not convinced me. And I would not see him in person again. My tale would veer too far off course were I to detail the nuances of my own life which followed. Let it be known simply that I married, had children and enjoyed a fruitful life. The roots that grew from the hardened soil of my childhood village had provided adequate nourishment to the bloom that would be my adult life, and while a maudlin mood would settle upon me to recall that simpler time, I knew that I would always be invariably tied to that little old town. A man is so crucially shaped by moments early in life, and whether we realise them or not is each man's own story. Ashen would write to me over the years; I would always write back with vigour. It saddens me to say that he never left the old village, and his words would always fill me with a melancholy most difficult to shift. He would always claim of happiness, but just as an old friend should, I knew better. Even in the ink strokes of his letters I could feel the moribund core of his faded joy, as though the light in his eyes was slowly being extinguished through self-sabotage. His issues no longer encompassed that fateful encounter with the old hag at the carnival, rather they stemmed from it into a darker, more dreadful fear. Many have said that once one realises that they will die one day, their life will be richer (I most certainly echo these sentiments). For Ashen it had been a horrible opposite; the realisation that he would die, be it terribly or no, crippled the man's ailing momentum. His words belied this - why should he begin upon anything if all roads lead to death? Poor fool! If only he had listened; if only I had been more energetic in my chastising.

'And one day, he died. Just as he should have; just as any other man, he died. I am but an old codger now, and I wonder whether it could be considered 'jubilant' that he too lived to the age he did. Many would argue that to live to his age before passing is admirable, but the unsettling circumstances about his death - nay - his life filled me with awful forbearance. I would certainly have mourned for him immediately, had the announcement of his death not been so dismissive. A letter arrived from the village that all but skimmed over the fact. 'Some sad news on all fronts - Ashen has passed; your mother is very ill.' The letter was apparently intended to bring my attention to my dear old mother, who was apparently approaching her final days, and that I should come to see her one last time. With my father's passing a decade earlier she had none attending her. Naturally I obliged and set off home with that adrenalin-charged stupor that comes with the initial shock of grief. My movements were mechanical; the haze in which I wandered clouded all rational thought and stripped them down to their most bare motor skill. Ashen was dead, mother was soon to follow. And with this, the people I had known from my childhood were all gone - I was the last one left and would surely walk the valley myself soon. It was too much for me to comprehend.

'A distant cousin met me at the station. A kindly bloke, I must say; he reassured me that mother was comfortable and had some time yet. He wondered would I quickly attend to Ashen's will and testament before visiting mother, to which I stood with mouth agape.

"'Must it be myself who attends to this? What of his family?"

"'He'd none, sir," was the reply, "he lived alone for as long as I have known him. I was told you were a good friend of his."

"'But certainly," I stammered for words, "I have not spoken to him for years! Let alone seen the man!"

'My cousin shrugged - and what more did I expect him to do? He was but the messenger. Sympathetically I accepted the request upon the promise that mother would not mind waiting briefly.

'The sight of the room brought the first tears to my drought-stricken eyes. It was in the exact same state as it had been for decades. Nothing had changed save the thick coats of dust and crippling odour that cloaked the walls. Very much the hovel of a hermit it remained, loveless and cold. Books and papers littered the room, as though Ashen kept these as a single means of escapism.

'"I do hope he did not suffer."

'"I am afraid that is unlikely, I have heard that poisoning is a dreadful way."

'"Poison?! Then he has been murdered?"

'"With all due respect sir, it appears to have taken his life."

'I felt as though struck by a sledgehammer.

'"I am very sorry to be the one to tell you all this. Hopefully all is explained in the will. Can I assist you in anything?"

'I took a moment before answering, "N-no. No that is fine. If you could just grant me a minute or two alone?"

'My cousin nodded swiftly and removed himself from the room. The silence that followed his egress cut me to the heart, and all at once a wretched sobbing overcame me. Poor Ashen! To take his own life of all things! When I was at last able to compose myself, I moved toward his writing desk, upon which a single envelope lay exempt from the mindless clutter of papers about the rest of the room. It was as if this envelope repelled its other brethren, sitting there as it were, stark white against the mahogany writing desk. Considering its important contents, it was a rather weightless letter, and I was a little shocked to find only a single leaf of paper within it. I remember feeling that perhaps it would indeed be a short will, for Ashen had apparently fallen from contact with all others. To encapsulate my horror at reading this paper would be impossible; may I say simply that my heart swelled with intense terror that held me paralysed to the spot. A sentence. One awful sentence marked the letter, written in a hurried and frantic penmanship.

'*Somebody help me.*

'The raw and sickening dismay was all too much to bear. Those awful words, not uttered, but penned in a moment of utmost distress - the old hag had been right! The letter fell from my shaking hands and I too followed it to the floor, my knees giving way beneath me I collapsed to the floor. My cousin, hearing the thud of my fall, raced to my side, where the poor fellow tried desperately to console me. He did not understand the weight of my grief, the magnitude of what I had just experienced, and could do no more but grasp me in his arms as I wept. Time was still; how many minutes passed before I could compose myself, I do not know. In the end, all that could move me was the reminder that I had to go see my mother.

'The sight of her calmed me, and I was once again like an infant in her soothing presence. She sat comfortably in her bed, apparently doing nothing but wearing upon her face a most contented smile - a smile that spoke of a life fulfilled in so little words - I knew she was happy and well accepting of her own fate. Lo! To picture her now, sitting there an extreme opposite to poor old Ashen! How strange our reactions to death's inevitability!

'"You look like you've seen a ghost, dear! Surely your mother does not look so awful?"

'Her voice was slow and quiet, and again the tears welled in my eyes, "It is so good to see you."

'I saw then the struggle she faced so bravely; stoic as she was, it clearly pained her to talk too much. Still she spoke, "I am terribly sorry to hear of old Ashen. Your childhood friend - I know the grief you must feel."

'"Little are its barbs, mother," I replied, "when faced with the impending loss of one dearer."

'"You should not grieve too long, my boy. You and I both know I am in the Lord's hands. I welcome his approach."

'"Brave woman! Such faith is admirable. But Ashen, I fear I may have done more to help him."

'"You did what was asked of you as his friend. There is little else to do when one's ears are not open to listen. Ashen allowed himself to become obsessed with things that were out of his control. He *chose* to listen to that senile old woman."

'I started, "You knew of that fateful visit?"

'"Of course," she replied, "I have lived here my entire life - as did Ashen - he spoke of little else. Refused to listen even to me who had been like a mother to him."

'"The clairvoyant…."

'"Pah! Psychics? Mediums? The woman was a wanderer, a rambler - *a renowned charlatan*. I knew her briefly in my youth. She once lived in the village. A nasty one, to be sure, the lies she would spin more intricate than the spider's web."

'"I can't believe you knew the woman."

'"She herself was banished from the village. You know the superstitious bunch that has lived here. Fact of the matter is she was nothing more than a trickster, but Ashen would not believe otherwise. I am sure she must have told that same awful story to all of her patrons."

'Here I wept anew. So the gypsy had been a farce! Ashen had crafted his own demise out of fear and paranoia. The gypsy had merely planted the seed of doubt, while Ashen had nourished it! What tragic irony that my friend would deny the benevolent Lord as a faerie tale, yet be tricked by superstitious nonsense! He, the stoic atheist, unshakable in his resolution, befallen by a sleight of hand, a magician's trick! I have said before that I have lived a most satisfactory life, yet this tragedy truly stuck, truly stood out as one regret I could not appease. Am I a fool to have not helped him more? Surely there was little more I could have done.

Could one blame the old hag? She was merely a storyteller, with Ashen just another spectator in her sideshow. Perhaps - and alas that I must say this - Ashen is the one truly at fault. He was a fool to have become obsessed with things beyond his control. In the end all involved have had to learn the hard way that a man must die, and what lies beyond that black curtain will forever be a mystery to our waking reality. God, gild me for the road ahead; I feel it sometimes better to shut one's ears and move silently, for such matters as life after death and foretelling of the future are much too opaque for man to ever understand fully.'

A Strange Thing Happens

When Iggy Oberon finished his story, silence pervaded. The children sat slack-jawed and enthralled, the audience had increased from just Mutt and Churl as word got around that Uncle Iggy was telling a tale. The wind cut past and sent Mutt into a shiver – a goose must have walked over his grave – that's what his mama would say. The mid-morning hadn't revealed itself through sunlight, and the sky remained overcast, teasing at rain that probably wouldn't fall. The frost had dissipated but the hearts of those who had listened to Iggy had been chilled.

"What happened to the old lady?" whispered Churl.

"Who can tell?" replied Iggy, "But mind you – though she may have gone done a rotten thing by poor Ashen, her words carried a warning!"

Rosie, who had hitherto been beating the dust from various articles of clothing, tutted crankily, "Now why d'you go telling them about such things? 'Tis an harsh topic, Ig. No child should know have to it."

"Aww don't be sore, Rosie. Better they hear of the nasty stuff from a trusted old friend like as me."

"Hmm, I don't like it, Iggy. They're just children. I'll be awaking ya if any of them come to me with nightmares."

In a foolish risk, Iggy decided to test her ire, "Your Aunt Rosie misses the point, kiddies. It's the ugly things in life that remind us of the pretty things. See the world kids, don't just stay here ya whole lives."

Rosie looked sternly at Iggy but softened when she saw the apologetic look on his face. It might be crocodile tears but she knew that Iggy Oberon was generally well-meaning. Truth be known the man himself certainly hoped he didn't give anybody bad dreams. No, she'd drop it for now, but he'd have it coming once she caught him alone.

"I think Uncle Iggy also means," she said, "that stories might be true or fake, but either way ye can walk away from it and don't let nothing trouble ya."

"Yer that'll do it, Rose!"

At that moment Stymphales, all covered in feathers, came lurching down the main street of the shanty town. Iggy saw him from a distance, cheeks flushed and glistening with a cold sweat. On any other day this would be about the time Stymphales returned from the fields, before the sun got too hot, but there was something about his quickened gait that raised an immediate concern.

"Stymphales, you lout. I just dust and you come in kicking it all up again." Rosie scolded.

The newcomer stopped and gasped for air with hands on knees, the feathery tunic clinging to his well-formed chest. The mayor Coldchop who had remained silent until this point, sighed audibly; in spite of his own doughy and shapeless body, he thought that *surely their young hunters had better fitness than this?*

"Did you wake a drowsy bear or something, mate? Where's Artemis?" asked Iggy.

"Something so strange happens now," said Stymphales, "Arty is where it's at. Reckon you should come look."

"It must be the rain! My dance worked!" cried Coldchop, "Let us go immediately! Lead the way!"

"Mr. Chop, if you pleases," quipped Stymphales, "it is a fair walk. I'd suggest our stronger folk Iggy and Thorn."

"Pah! Suit yourselves then. Tell ya though – come back empty-handed and me grumbling stomach will send you deaf!"

Iggy Oberon stood and threw his stock hat onto his head, "Reckon you'll survive a meal skipped, Choppy," and to Thorn-Petal he cried, "How about it, Thornie? Up for a romantic walk?"

"Dream on, Oberon. But I'll assist if you keep yer mouth shut along the way."

Mutt, Churl and the other chillun leapt as one with pleading faces. Something strange was happening, something exciting; after Iggy's story they wanted to embark on their own adventures, and whatever Stymphales had discovered might be the perfect start.

"Naw, kiddies, I'm in enough trouble already," here Iggy winked at Rosie, "Why don't ya help your Aunties in the fields however you can."

Strapping a small scythe to her hip, Thorn-Petal smiled to hear the collective groan of the young ones. There had been enough excitement for them for one day. But as for Stymphales, it was clear that he was impatient to leave and, kicking the dust from his shoe and champing down onto a piece of grass, Iggy followed after him with Thorn-Petal close by.

Away from the shanty town there was little that could protect against the wild elements. Silence pervaded, yet any sound that was roused from the brown earth – the snap of a twig, the cry of a bird or the whistle of the wind – seemed amplified against that echoing quiet. The Ochre Magpies, whose piebald pelts made them blend in with the dirty ground, cawed with anti-social abandon. They knew the men who walked through here would often shoot at them with slingshots, and the birds felt their revenge fulfilled in the stealing of random items from the shanty town. Indeed, Iggy and Thorn-Petal saw more of the rusted tin can men in pieces around the magpie nests, some bird houses held together with string and clothes pegs that Rosie had used in her own nesting. A static crunched through the air, making Iggy feel uneasy, and Thorn-Petal chopped through charred underbrush with her scythe; in a few months there might be a fresh bloom of green on the eucalypt trunks, but while the bush remained burnt out from recent wild fire, nothing would grow. Once again, the overwhelming sense of death cloaked the Mid-North, in this place where no trains passed through, and even the radio tower signals failed to reach.

Stymphales remained a considerable distance in front, turning his head now and then to confirm that they were still following. He was normally an excitable young man, but today his energy bordered on feverish; Iggy hoped nothing bad had happened to Artemis. Thorn-Petal strode with a determination native to her person, and in due time the triad reached a small clearing in the form of an impact crater. Such abnormalities in the terrain were fairly common in the Mid-North. Some theorised that the comets that had struck the earth however long ago were responsible for the inhibited plant growth in the region, but maybe that was just an old-wives' tale. This particular crater dipped steeply into the red soil and had become inundated with underbrush and brambles. Gnarled roots shot from the clay walls having expected to spread themselves further but instead found themselves shivering in the open air of the crater. Iggy saw Artemis immediately, squatted as she was at the bottom of the dip analysing an indiscernible shadow beneath her. Iggy and Thorn-Petal sat upon the rim of the crater and slid down on their rumps, while the more adroit Stymphales leapt down fragile footholds. Before they reached Artemis, Iggy could see what she was examining; the curious bundle at her feet was in fact another person, unconscious by the look of things.

"One of ours?" asked Thorn-Petal.

Artemis rose to her full height, she was a tall woman with straw-coloured hair faded against her pale skin – she lacked shadow and contour, leaving her somewhat unremarkable of face, "No," she replied plainly.

Iggy knelt by the dreary stranger – a young woman by the looks of things – and brushed a limp strand of auburn hair from her face. Her garb was most unusual for one of the Mid-North; in fact, Iggy would have guessed it to be a mariner's uniform and, adding further to the bizarreness of the situation, the tattered clothes were covered in seaweed as if the woman had just washed ashore on a barren beach.

"She's stirring," said Thorn-Petal.

Indeed, the girl coughed and revived, by the time she opened her eyes she had the same look of bewilderment as the four strangers who stood over her.

"… Shore," she whispered, "I've found the shore."

Iggy looked at Thorn-Petal who shrugged.

"Ain't no shore here, love. You're in the Mid-North. Jesus nowhere."

"How, where are my mates?"

"Nobody else here, sweetie," said Thorn-Petal, "you got a name?"

The strange girl furrowed her brow as if struggling to remember, "Ivy. My name is Ivy."

Gull & Leviathan – A Fable

As transcribed ad nauseum by Delaney Vespers:

White bird, he flew across the blue
To desolation's shore.
'Cross peaks of stone that cloak their bones
with iron shrub and hoar.

About the coast of island ghosts
Did flutter that lone 'gull
He spotted then leviathan –
And perched on living hull.

With water spout spoke mighty trout,
"Why comest thou to me?
My back you greet with combing feet
As though I were your tree."

Stately gull, puffed up and full,
Bespake as claimant then,
"Far I've flown, that I might own
The hills of Kerguelen.

My brothers' song, forever long
Is what I flew to flee.
Their prattling tide made me decide
There are no gulls like me."

Spake again, Leviathan
"Why comest thou to me?
You see me doze within the throes
Of icy reverie."

"To purge that din, a horrid sin —
Birdsong of avian!
Long I yearn for taciturn
Delights of Kerguelen."

Spake again, Leviathan
"Why comest thou to me?
Thy weathered plight, thy feathered flight
Does not relate to me."

"Mistake me not, thou patriot,
I am not here for thee.
I'd thought this place bereft of face —
Alone, I came to be."

Spake again, Leviathan,
"Thou art a thoughtful bird.
How comest thou to disavow
What kin hath ne'er heard?

Fool adrift — go mend this rift!
Do as your kin would do.
Turn back again from whence thou came,
This clime is not for you.

Thy treasure, lo! Thy pleasure, oh!
To be part of a flock.
I am but one, my friends — I've none
Around this dismal rock."

"Oh giant fish, just hear my wish
Pray don't proclaim me rude.
Though here be few, thou knows that two
Can't share of solitude."

Spake again, Leviathan,
"Then thou must leave me be."
Then gull took wing and fish did fling
Itself into the sea.

Leviathan of Kerguelen
Swam round his claimed land.
He'd soon derive birds can't survive
Beyond those blackened sands.

White bird, he flew across the blue
Away from that bleak shoal.
Away from peaks to search and seek
With silent south the goal.

But Winter rose and wings they froze –
Snow drifts but his flock's twin.
And he in white was lost from sight,
Just as he once had been.

Holes in the History of Things

Patience; it was always patience with Delaney Vespers. The pen dropped from her cramped hand and she flexed it to get the blood flowing once more. It was ten o'clock and Delaney had scribed *Gull & Leviathan* five times – past the halfway mark but not nearly good enough if she were to finish her punishment before bed. Sleep would have to be compromised at this rate – not a big deal given the somewhat lax life of a student with no bills, mortgages or other worldly responsibilities; yet in the eyes of Vespers, like any lethargic teenager the thought of sleep deprivation sung a bitter nocturne in her heart. Her head ached in the warm night; the last of the straggling students who were enjoying the evening outside had begun to turn themselves in. A few stray moths flitted lazily about the chandelier in her dorm, their dust-coated wings scattering flakes onto the cobwebbed fixture. It was a luxuriant looking thing to have in hanging in a simple student's lodge, but that was just the way of Calumnia. Vespers didn't care much for it, for it represented the very hypocrisy she cried out against. A pig in a suit was still a pig – as was her dorm more akin to a cell no matter how opulent it appeared. All of these student 'cells' were fitted with those chandeliers, the walls built with flint and sandstone – offcuts from the mines of Cardinal Mons. Her bunk was cramped at best; each student could lay claim to one thin slab of a mattress as well as a small writing desk, and pertaining to these humble lodgings and the hot evening, sleep would be tough to wrangle anyway. Maybe it was better that she was still awake and writing lines.

Delaney's desk was cluttered – too cluttered to be of use to her at present, and in all honesty, she preferred to do her writing on her bed, lying flat on her stomach and propped up by her elbows. There was a comforting quality to it, seeing her books and pens all lined out in front of her, ready at any time to be plucked into her grasp and utilised. She found herself musing over *Gull & Leviathan*, pondering its bizarre and unknown origins; even those snoots who call themselves teachers at Calumnia had no idea of its date of writing or its author. But then again there were holes in the history of things – such timid resolution toward the unknown was accepted continent-wide by many of the great minds. Things 'we simply do not know' as those minds would say. Delaney loved to hear that line; to her, it brought those educational snobs back down to earth. In her mind, the world would never be completely understood, not by humanity at least – people were far too minute to have the world's origins revealed to them. Most of the recorded history seemed to trace back to a certain point known as the Cataclysm – some moment along the path of time where the records suddenly stopped, leaving anything that came prior deep in an unknowable past. Occasionally some artefact would arise to reveal a tantalizing insight into the unobtainable knowledge – a song perhaps, or a manuscript, even things like words and expressions – things with no recorded origin, and those that might have laid claim to such treasures could never prove themselves completely. To Delaney Vespers, they were adornments to a world of fantasy, decorations on a tree that had no scientific name because it did not exist in this time. Mythical places like Orstraylia, Rusha, Yoorop; songs about 'star men' and 'fascination streets'; even poems like *Gull & Leviathan*.

Some said that the Cataclysm was the beginning; that it set the natural order of the world into motion, but like all beliefs on the subject that was only an opinion. How could such a thought explain away the remains of that alien past? Delaney thought that to call them 'holes in history' was an utter cop-out; she liked to believe that there had been a fantastic world that existed before the Cataclysm, one she could never know, but could visit in her wildest fantasies. The great unknown fascinated her, and this was another reason why *Gull & Leviathan* intrigued her so. Maybe that poem by a nameless author held a clue to the creation of the world! Delaney liked to think as such, but most scholars believed it was probably just some remnant of little significance. So why study it? Well that was merely due to its status as an unknown artefact; the fact that it seemed to predate much of recorded history piqued the interest of scholars, so much so that the poor students of Calumnia were doomed to study its archaic words as part of the curriculum.

By now Delaney had scribed the poem seven times and sighed in the aching heat of the evening. There was less light now; the lamps outside on the grounds had been extinguished for the night, and the halls had been dimmed in a subtle way that informed the students that it was time to sleep. The cicadas sung their monotonous note to the starless sky, a din broken by a sudden gasping sound – a snort of sorts – and Delaney looked down at the bottom bunk and saw her roommate Odina sleeping in a bedraggled mess. Delaney shook the haze from her tired head; she had not heard Odina come in, but now that her roommate had begun to snore loudly, she realised the struggle she faced if she were to concentrate long enough to scribe the poem three more times. Again, Delaney Vespers mused on the words (she was usually quite proud of her own neat handwriting) and considered the land of Kerguelen – whether it had in fact ever existed or whether it was a figment more akin to Atlantis. Either way, its cold shorelines sounded like a welcome reprieve to the warm night at Calumnia, and sent the train of Vespers thoughts the way of a confirmed wonderland, of *Ultima Thule*.

Verdigris – the Continent had long been the only hospitable landmass in the world, but that did not mean there weren't other great landmasses floating about the vast oceans. The students had recently learnt of Maree Bird Land – an icy expanse far south of Verdigris. But Ultima Thule – as the scholars titled it – was a land long known, yet seen only by a few foolhardy sailors who'd seen its shores and returned to tell of it. The barren and rocky coast of this unconquerable land stretched for untold miles some months' worth of sailing from the safety of Verdigris' green country. Even with new technology shortening the leagues betwixt the two landmasses, the great minds were no closer to understanding Ultima Thule and whether it could be put to use in some way by the human race. It gave off the impression of being impossibly big – far larger in its expanse than Verdigris – yet only a few explorers had ventured further than a few miles inland before they would either vanish entirely or return savagely mutated. *Cursed Soil* was the name given by those adventurers; the earth of that isolated wasteland was poisonous, thunderstruck and utterly infertile. Its savage mountains warned shore-bound intruders with their dominant height, telling them quite frankly that *there was nothing for them here* through loveless crags and wild winds. How far did Ultima Thule expand? How much of the world was under rule of its toxic tendrils? Could life flourish beyond its shores? Was there hope of another land much like Verdigris beyond that apocalyptic barrier? These were the questions that had haunted the dreams of philosophers and scientists alike – and curse man's short few decades on the earth! If only the brightest minds had a few short centuries to themselves, perhaps those mysteries would be revealed! Alas, many minds had been and gone and still humanity was no closer to understanding the limits of the world they lived in.

Odina snorted loudly and Delaney snapped back into reality. She began to scribble once more, but by the time she'd scribed *'White bird he flew,'* her pen failed on her and no amount of shaking it in her fist would get it working again. The snoring of her roommate reached an intolerable volume and Delaney huffed and threw her broken pen to the floor. It clinked noisily on the flagstones, causing Odina to stir – yet she did not wake. Delaney threw her head over the side of the bunk and observed the lump of sheets housing that beastly snoring; she shouted – to no response. Grabbing the edges of her mattress Delaney shook the bed frame – still Odina slept. Finally, seeing no other option, Delaney Vespers leapt to the floor with a thud and pinched her roommate's nose.

"Wake up,"

"I left it on the desk!" Odina burst suddenly into waking.

"What?"

"I did my homework, ma'am. It's on your – huh?"

"Wake up, Odina," said Delaney, "I wanna go to the library. Come with?"

With hair shaken by sleep strung over her bird-like face, Odina looked rather comical, and she grunted angrily upon this disturbance of slumber. Then, like a landslide, she slipped easily back into a doze; before Delaney could realise, the sound of snores once more echoed in the tiny room.

"Hey!" she shouted.

Odina shot upright, "It's the middle of the night! Go away!"

"There's something I want to look up. Come with me; I don't want to go alone," said Delaney and, seeing Odina's hesitation, added, "I'll give you my breakfast tomorrow?"

This seemed to grab Odina's attention; she sat up and rubbed the sleep from her eyes, "What about your detention? They'll make you write lines again if we get caught – and I'll get dragged into it too!"

But Odina had seemingly made her decision, standing slowly from her bunk and throwing on a light coat. When there was a second breakfast involved, detention might be worth it. Lord knew the meal portions at Calumnia were impossibly small.

"Ultima Thule!" said Delaney.

"What?" winced Odina, "don't push it, Vespers."

"Alright, alright, I'll stop. Thanks for coming."

"Whatever,"

The two girls slipped into the halls, Delaney clasping a small lantern aloft. Odina muttered behind her with grumbling protests were matched only by the rumble of her stomach – but at least the promise of a free breakfast would quash that complaint.

Mawson's Journal

As read by Delaney Vespers in the shadows of the school library, late in the evening:

Some 1200 nautical miles north west of Desolation Cove.

Embarked a fortnight ago. Hustle upon the ship and a severe case of gout preventing me from logging here until now. It is already a dreary voyage, the sea pitches us about so with swell to sicken even the more experienced men onboard. Haven't seen a seagull in days, nor any marine life, and only now do I realise the effect such simple creatures can have on a man's morale. Even the dogs are restless, oft unwilling to play with the men for preference of cowering below deck. I fear this voyage may have been doomed from the beginning after young Bellingham was killed at weigh anchor. Foolish lad had an accident loading the cargo deck and tipped overboard, clipped the dock edge on the way down and split his head clean apart. His brother still grieves - rightly so - and has not been right of mind in his maritime duties. The business of it all can conflict with a man's sense of decency; the boy should have been relieved of duty, but the voyage couldn't be delayed for the sake of one deckhand. Yet it's these hard decisions that weigh on my conscience, for while the Second Mate of the ship must carry on, myself, Mawson - but a man - wish I could pay proper respect to the perished lad and his family. Money talks, so they say, and far too much has been banked on the success of this voyage. Captain Byrd informed me that the nuances of our journey had reached the very top of Magna Luxuria, and at my age I must say I don't enjoy that kind of pressure placed upon my station. Nonetheless we press on, making handsome time enroute to that great unknowable continent. We make for Ultima Thule.

One day later.

Of course, I knew the legends surrounding it. As a boy one would dabble in extravagant fantasies of far-off worlds, of civilisations not yet known and treasures unlike anything found on our own continent. Factual history being scarce, we've been left to revel as babes and fill out the gaps with our own hypotheses.

Two weeks later.

Lost another man today. A ship hand again; by the name of Falconer. Stood too close to a boiler exhaust and was blasted by steam pouring from the flue. Our pursuit of mastering technology we don't yet understand was this poor soul's undoing; voyages of this kind, with this craft, are new, and as such we've yet to establish proper safety regulations. Common sense might have saved him, but I can forgive the man for not understanding the machines he was working with. Severe steam burns, he is unlikely to recover. His mate Amund, barely a teen, is distraught with the accident and suffers greatly.

One and a half months later.

Our trajectories indicate we are most likely a week away from our fabled shoreline. Today brought with us a bizarre phenomenon; we were beset by the most curious starfish one could lay eyes upon. Davis spotted them in the dawning from his perch in the crow's nest. The ocean had been mysteriously still that eve, no breath of wind tarnished the reflections of stars upon the millpond surface. But it was once the sky lightened with the orange of dawn that the stars were drowned from view, yet the 'reflections' remained. We realise now that we must have been in the company of the strange starfish for some time before we noticed their presence. They were everywhere, surrounding the ship in their thousands, and to look upon them one might not immediately discern anything awry, anything different to a starfish one might find on the beach at home. Davis and Casey brought a few of the creatures aboard using our nets, and we all gathered around to take a look for ourselves (such has been our desperate isolation from humanity that we crave anything new to break the monotony of sailing). Although the starfish possessed no face, no obvious physical indicator of emotion, they jostled affectionately on our outstretched arms, their cool skin icy to the touch, as though their blood were quicksilver, and the barb-like protrusions on their limbs yielded to our prodding like rubber. And they were of the most iridescent colours; all the spectrum dotted those lovely shapes, shapes that hint at a more cosmic origin. I cannot explain why the men found these creatures so fascinating. It is perhaps a childish affliction that we all felt our spirits uplifted with our little friends, the starfish - not unlike a rhyme one remembers from the sepia echoes of time long past; their shape and colour like a birdsong amongst the funeral dirge of our drab and dreary voyage. Certainly the *esprit de corps* that has developed in the men gives me hope that our journey may be successful after all.

Four days later.

The sea remains still, but our progress has slowed to a crawl. The starfish have disappeared and in their place the water is inundated with a thick aquatic weed. This presence of plant life must mean the outward slog of our long journey is reaching its end. Normally sightings as such give me a lightness of the chest, a sort of tension release at the thought of *terra firma* beneath my feet. But it was the slowness of travel combined with the awful properties of the weed that I instead felt a return of that foreboding that plagued the early days of the voyage. The prow cut through weed and water, the former being of a putrid black colour and a consistency so sluggish that we may have been sailing through tar. Again, we used the nets to bring some of the weed aboard, and the ship's botanist Mr Solander assessed it with a same vigour in which he studied our starfish companions. He found the plant to be unlike anything found at home; holding to the shape of common seaweed, until the slightest contact would break it apart. It would congeal loosely back together to its original shape as though held together by a weak magnetism. And not to mention the smell - such foetid odour deserves a sentence of its own - well, even our hardiest men pitched their shoulders overboard and vomited gracelessly into the sea.

So too, our first sighting of avian species brought unease descending on us as the silent air was cut by a most dreadful raven-like caw in the morn's early hours. We saw shadows of creatures circling above, and as the sun rose behind the cloud cover to bring the grey of an overcast morning, we observed strange cormorants fishing in the putrid waters of weed. Their down was of a course brown with leathery wings not unlike a bat, and they would plunge aggressively beneath the water's surface and emerge coated in the sickly weed I described earlier. Surely some creature lurked below and served as their prey, for thick bubbles burst betwixt weeds; here and there a fin or tail slapped anonymously in the filth. And unlike the starfish, these birds kept their distance, eyeing us off with midnight black eyes like an opposing army standing at a distance. The way they observed us - cold, hostile (and perhaps fearful?) - meant that the first sight of land was met with unease. Certainly, we had some relief - none more so than Byrd, whose shoulders dropped with a sigh as Casey yelped of his findings from the crow's nest. Indeed, there it was, stretching as far as East does to West - the coastline of Ultima Thule. Its jagged outline cut the horizon like a saw; the peaks were curiously symmetric to a certain degree, like teeth in the same rotted mouth appear differently sized but somehow similar. On occasion there came a silent flicker of lightning over the summits, with no thunder accompanying those menacing flashes. The men were left to enjoy this light show whilst Captain Byrd rowed ashore with two of his swabbies. Our ship bobbed in the shallows like a piece of rotten fruit, with the sluggish wake plopping against the hull ad nauseum, and all we could do was wait. Byrd wanted to determine the most suitable place to drop anchor - somewhere we could pitch up camp and recoup before the next stage in our journey. I must admit a level of scepticism on my part at this point; the shoreline met us with saw-toothed rocks and oyster-sharp cliff faces. Even the sand of the beaches carried a drab sediment that left the line between land and shallows blurred with dirt and darkness.

We waited until a powdery dusk descended before Captain Byrd returned, his lantern cutting swathes through the light fog surrounding. The lightning continued intermittently, and not a sound broke the silence bar the slapping of oars. Byrd's face was drawn and frustrated; the coast remained the same up and down for miles. No cove or bay would welcome us it seemed, as though this dreaded continent met us with a phalanx formation of rock and peaks. Verily the coast was straight and unchanging in this section of Ultima Thule, and we knew nothing of its outer perimeters. It was decided that we would drop anchor right where we were, and the men, some more eager than others, unloaded our stores into the boats and rowed ashore.

One day later

Camp brought some merriment, if only for an evening. By the time the sun had rose and set again the reality of the rather inhospitable place dawned upon us. We will need to hurry if we're to find the missing crew, or discern any new information about Ultima Thule, for a rather simple reason - *there is no food anywhere*. We must rely only on our provisions. There was not a tree or plant anywhere, no mollusc or barnacle clung to any rock, no fish disturbed our hooks. Some of the boys managed to knock one of those cormorants from the sky and bludgeon it to death, however they found the beast had little meat, and those who tried to eat it retched horribly, and have spent the day adding their own brown water to the landscape. Byrd called me and first mate McMurdo to his tent, where we discussed a plan of action. He reiterated our objective of finding a trace of Captain North's expedition and to bring back with us any items of interest with which to study back at port. He made sure we knew of the struggled we faced - we had no map of this place, for all we knew we were one of the first people to tread here - and of North's crew, we had nothing to go on except a faint distress signal that had mysteriously weakened the closer we got to Ultima Thule. I expressed my concern that North's signal might be interfered with by the excessive lightning about this place, which Byrd agreed albeit crestfallen. And making matters worse was a discovery none of us could have foretold, and no doubt a matter that may have played part in the lost expedition's plight - *our compasses are useless here*. A glance upon their faces saw the needle indecisively move this way this way and that - never settling on a confirmed north point (and only now do I realise the irony of such a thing - given we are looking for the man named North). Nevertheless, we had the distress signal to guide us, and we sanctioned off stores with which to make supply caches to distribute on our journey inland - however far that might stretch. Despite our efforts to persuade him otherwise, Captain Byrd will be part of the team to trek in the direction of the signal, with myself joining him. McMurdo implored our leader to remain in camp on the shore, lest some ill fate befall him, but Byrd resolutely refuted it; McMurdo was to oversee the base and await our return. Five of us would make up the party - Byrd; our strong men Davis and Casey; Byrd's swabbie, Finch; and myself. And one must not omit mention of Daisy, one of the dogs still with us, who would also accompany us.

Next day

Much passed today. Our quintet embarked on our inland journey under the grey light of dawn, yoked to our packs like beasts of burden. Granted, our load will be lighter in time as we deposit caches for the return trip. Our only means of following the distress signal is through use of a very expensive piece of equipment entrusted to us by the Magna Austrinus militia; it behaves somewhat like a radio or a telephone - a small boxed speaker with a single antenna. Byrd himself would carry the trinket, and to be fair none of us wanted to shoulder the responsibility of misplacing or breaking the thing. Lord knows this diary of paper and pen has made my position on advanced technology utterly clear. And thus, our steady trudging across the crags was accompanied by a maddening drone of sound, comparable but lower than a mosquito whine, or a pair of cello strings vibrating a tritone. It was a nauseating din, one that we men couldn't seem to drown out amongst the wailing of winds and occasional cracks of thunder. The distress signal played on our temperaments, distracted us, left us irritable and sometimes indecisive; it was a most awful feeling, one that is difficult to explain as I write. Thankfully the radio can be switched off to give us a reprieve, and we soon made it habit to discern the direction where the signal was loudest, then turn the thing off while we marched, checking periodically to ensure we hadn't strayed. Two caches stored today, would estimate a total of twenty miles walked. Must preserve ink, and sleep calls me.

Three more days later

What can be said of our environs? This is a dreadful place; the unusual phenomena are mounting too. We are all of the conclusion that *Ultima Thule behaves under its own set of physics*. Beyond our compasses spinning uselessly, the fundamentals we as humanity plant our very feet upon are wildly altered on these shores. The air is dry, yet the ground feels moist - as such our fires are difficult to start; once they are going, they behave as strangely as our compasses, tossing flames about in seemingly intelligent patterns, and they are unaffected by even strong winds. Casey cut himself on a jagged handhold and found his spilled blood congealed on the rocky surface until the droplets sat like beads - the earth itself appears to reject our very fibres (not to mention offering us nothing in way of nourishment). The birds are gone, and no other sign of life emerges on this barren land. Worse still, Finch has fallen ill, and slows our progress (forgive me for doubting the lad's vigour, but clearly the proof is on show). Day brings no sun; night brings no moons or stars; nothing guides us but the signal. The cloud cover hangs like a blanket across the shoulders of the crags, and lightning strikes are the only movement we observe. Byrd becomes restless; we've trekked days yet seem no closer to finding the source of the distress signal, or North's expedition. The drone of the radio is unwavering, and we have marched mostly straight and to the north. But who could say what kind of progress we'd made? My skills in cartography are futile when there are no distinct landmarks to record. The boys' morale is beginning to fall, and Daisy can bring no cheer. She paces along with us, and even when we camp for the nights, she is restless. We need something soon, something that encourages us, lets us know we are closer to our goal. Why does nothing change in this bloody place? The thunder claps indifferently.

Two? days later (can't remember)

Something changed today. It was subtle, much like our encounter with the starfish - that of a mysterious blue mineral speckled in the fissures and outcrops of dark brown rock. It was rather bright looking stuff and reflected the dull grey light of the sky in shimmers of azure and cobalt. Those sections of rock where it lay embedded were smooth to the touch betwixt the harsh rock surrounding. Given our pace had slowed to a crawl, Byrd called for us to stop and examine the strange mineral. It was unlike any substance known to us, perhaps closest in appearance to a shell of Paua or any other pearl-like trinket one might find on a beach back home. We'd no geologist amongst the crew (and why would we?) but thought perhaps that our botanist Solander might find it interesting to study. That we had discovered some interesting material that we could bring with us back home was somewhat uplifting, for that had been a part of our original briefing. Satisfaction in our accomplishment was short-lived however, for we soon realised another whining cry out above the noise of the distress signal; Daisy whimpered pathetically at some spot several metres from us, and inspection of the source of her distress brought a horror we were not prepared for. The bitch had found a human femur; there was no denying it - the shape, size and presence of a scrap of cloth wrapped around it... *A human had perished here.*

Our initial reaction was one of sick shock, especially young Finch, whose illness left him weak and weary. But Byrd pulled us back like any good leader - for though we'd made a most upsetting discovery, this bone must have meant North's crew might be nearby. We pocketed the bone as well as handfuls of the blue mineral and pressed on. The men are tired, and all of us are feeling a peculiar illness, but we cannot stop now. We must be close.

(No date recorded)

We must abort our mission and return to the coast. There has been no further sighting of human presence since our run-in with the leg bone. Whatever befell North's expedition, we will not uncover on this voyage. Ever since our discovery of the blue mineral we have all descended gradually into a sickness that has crippled those of us remaining - I say remaining, for Finch has died. He woke us last night with awful spasms, thrashing about the tents like a drowning man and screaming a most blood-chilling roar. The poor lad had been in terrible shape the entire mission, and whatever it is that ails the rest of us has become his demise. We had wanted to transport his body back to the shore for a proper burial (for our shovels are not strong enough to turn the earth on which we tread), but the boys and I are too weak to do so. Byrd coughs blood while I myself am plagued with a dreadful itching and dryness of skin. Davis complains of headaches while Casey strangely enough is physically sound, but cries uncontrollably with bitter anguish - his eyes glassy as though blind. Forgive us, Finch. You deserved a better send-off than you received. Please forgive us.

(No date recorded)

Disaster. Upon reaching our first supply cache, we found it to be empty. How? This is impossible. Curse the trickery of Ultima Thule! What is this place?! Damned be anyone who steps foot here. Nothing good can come of this land, I am certain we tread on accursed ground. There are things man is not meant to learn, and I fear we have become trapped by such things. Casey collapsed in wretched sobs today and would travel no further. We pleaded with him to continue, for we could not carry him ourselves, but there was no getting through to him. He flailed his arms and legs violently whenever one of us approached, and we had no choice but to leave him behind to his own devices. I feel cowardly for doing as such but the lives of many trump the life of one, I feel I've hinted at this in an earlier entry.

(No date recorded)

Cap's dead. Davie is dead.

Was just me and the little bitch for a while.

She turned on me today and tried to attack.

Shot her. Had no other choice. Dog meat is horrible. But I don't have any other food.

Surely not too much further to the coast. Must relay our findings, our fates, our discoveries. I'm the only one left, I can't give up.

The itch is unbearable. I'm bleeding everywhere. It leaks through my pores like sweat. I hate this place. I had my suspicions that this expedition was doomed from the start. But it was nothing more than intuition, and for whatever stupid fucking reason, man tends to ignore whatever he can't measure. Well I should have listened. My heart said no. But I kept going. I will probably die with this regret. To anyone who reads this - forget this place. We aren't meant to know it.

(A simple script, different to Mawson's hand)

25th

Should make port in a day or so. McMurdo gave me this thing to record here for the sake of completeness; he reckons someone will want to read it. Not sure why he picks me - never was good at me writing. Better than the other blokes though probably.

McMurdo, he took us home after we found this journal some five hundred metres from our camp on the shore. Some of the boys had grown concerned about Cap and those who'd trekked inland, and went on their own little wander around the camp outskirts to see if there were any sign of 'em. They'd been looking for a smoke signal, they says, until one of 'em stumbled onto Mawson's corpse. Heavy hearts all round when they came back with nothing but his bloodstained backpack. Some pretty rocks, that special radio they took, and this here journal; nothing else. Poor old Mawson was pretty thorough with his note taking. Makes my job easier, wrapping it all up good and proper.

45 of us embarked

7 deaths

39 of us return *(the number 38 is curiously scribbled out)*

We's all sick and sorry, our work's been sloppy on the way home. McMurdo is more concerned with getting home than following proper protocol anymore. Tis a bad feel, this trip. Something ain't right. We's sad to share of the deaths of our mates, but I tell ya there's a guilty part of us all that can't wait to be home.

Anyway, I reckon that's my job here done. I know I'm done, let me self-indulge here - I ain't sailing again. Not after that. Can't imagine what them blokes saw inland. That place was horrible. Could offer any pay you like and I still says no. The other men feel the same.

Impossible Patience

In the nights following the disappearance of his brother, Rheneas Woodnote experienced the same recurring dream. He was traipsing up the sandstone steps in a line with the Norfolk Wights - just another being tied to the chain gang. And there was his brother Balfour, always two places ahead of him, never turning to the sound of Rhen's voice, no matter how loud he shouted. Rheneas felt like he was underwater; his voice would make no sound, and his legs would try and kick away from the ghostly chain gang to no effect. Forced to climb up the hill repeatedly, Rheneas would feel the skin of his heels crack and still he would never be closer to his beloved brother. The ghosts would chant in that same awful manner, tense and Phrygian, their plainchant calling for rain so loudly that Rhen would cry for them to stop. When he raised his hands to cover his ears, he saw they were no longer there, as though his hands had been amputated as punishment for some sort of crime – the crime of letting his brother go missing. Like all of his dreams he tried to decipher a meaning from this nightly haunting but to little avail. The esoteric jumbles that his mind threw together made no sense at all, and he conceded that he must be experiencing shock from that traumatic evening.

The immediate aftermath of their botched attempt at ghostbusting had faded in his memory; perhaps Rhen's mind was deliberately trying to forget the fright of those horrid ghouls. However, the fallout that followed could not be ignored. Rheneas had not lied to his parents about the events of that night – there was no point in keeping anything a secret, and given the Norfolkian affliction to the supernatural, the encounter with the Wights was not scoffed at by anybody. Rhen's mother wept for days, his dad, with help from the townsfolk, scoured the rain-soaked hills for traces of his firstborn, and Rheneas was ordered to carry on with the menial tasks of daily life and await with hope that Balfour would appear somewhere. He would find his brother – he had to; it had been his idea to investigate the Wights; Balfour had only made it his own when he realised he might impress the young girl named Pidgee. Yet Rheneas would appear to sit idle, the hours wasting away in the classroom, attention barely focused on any school-related task at hand; Rhen knew that there was one almighty obstacle barricading the search for his brother. True to form the rain had returned to the town of Norfolk. For a fortnight after Balfour's vanishing, it fell in swathes. The Wights would not appear again until the blessings of a clear night fell upon that fateful hill. As such Rheneas was stricken with a most terrible impatience, a beast that suffocated the joy from his life and bound his arms and legs to inertness. And to what point could he pursue anything else whilst his brother remained unaccounted for? Several times Rheneas had tried to bring cheer to his household, but his parents grieved as though Balfour's disappearance had ensured his death.

No! It could not be possible! Rhen thought, *I will find him!*

He thought back to all the horror stories he'd read while nestled in the safety of his bedsheets; yes, whenever ghosts were a foot, there was always a logical reasoning behind them – to uncover that would be to find Balfour!

"Rheneas – stop this," his father barked, "Look at how upset your mother is."

The fish and potatoes before them were going cold; dinner had been side-tracked by an attack of grief striking Rhen's mother – such moments of inconsolability were becoming more frequent.

"If I go back to the hills on a clear night," continued Rheneas (almost to himself), "I'm sure I will discover something. Bal is okay, guys. I know it."

His father slammed his fist on the table, "Enough, boy! I'll have no more of this nonsense!"

His mother continued to sob as Rhen picked timidly at his food. He took a bite of fish and flinched, before removing a small bone from his mouth. Another bone; the standards he'd grown used to living in had certainly slipped. Being as young as he was, Rheneas didn't fully understand the magnitude of sorrow – especially that of losing a child – and as such saw the situation under a more impassive light. Why did mum keep crying? Dad's anger – why not focus more on finding Balfour? And if not, at least cook dinner properly! What good did crying ever do for anybody? In that moment the fish bone, the relentless rain that still fell, nobody to confide in – all these things left him completely frustrated.

"Another bone," he grumbled, testing his own bravery.

Instantly, Rheneas saw his mistake; his stomach dropped as his father raised his eyes to him with a look that could cut glass. Rhen hated himself for opening his mouth – he was in for it now.

"What was that?" his father growled.

"Nothing."

"Didn't sound like nothing. What have I told you about attitude?"

Rhen called upon another bout of adrenalin, rising from his chair with hands on his hips, "Balfour could be okay and you're just sitting here crying. Well, I've had enough!"

His mother spoke, "Wallace, Rhenny, please stop this,"

"You leave Balfour to the adults, Rhen," roared Wallace, "Don't meddle with things you can't understand. You're too young! And don't you dare speak to your mother like that."

Rheneas backed down into his chair.

"What your father is saying, dear," said his mother, wiping her face dry, "is that we need you to be a good boy right now. Don't be reckless. We don't know where Balfour is, but Lord if he turns up like that poor Figley boy -"

Her voice broke before she could finish and again she convulsed with sobs.

Again with Figley, thought Rheneas.

That boy had died accidently years ago, but in a small town, such tragedies sunk deep and were never too far from the edge of the mind – particularly for fretful parents wanting to remind their children to be behaved.

"That's got nothing to do with Bal, ma," said Rheneas, "Figley fell outta tree and cracked his head open!"

"Rheneas!" hissed his father.

"Point is, I'll find him, ma. Leave it to me, I just need one clear night to go to the hills."

His father pointed a finger right at him, "You will do no such thing. We may have lost one child. I will not lose you too."

Rhen's chin fell into his chest; he would argue no more. A part of him wanted to ark up again and boldly inform his father that *you can't stop me*, but one more look at his crying mother was enough for him to think otherwise.

The rest of their time spent at the table was silent but for the tearful sobbing of Rhen's mother. Rheneas slunk away and rinsed his plate 'like a good boy' and hurried upstairs to his bedroom. He heard the front door close – Wallace Woodnote defied the usual Norfolkian fear of darkness to steal another few hours searching for his son. The man hadn't slept much since the incident, none of them had really. Rhen lamented the rottenness of childhood; his internal yearning to be listened to was verging on moody adolescence – another developmental stage he had ahead of him to look forward to. Nobody took heed of a kid's words. Any wisdom he might lay claim to was trumped by age – *Sun been round me a few times more than you, boy* – Ah! That's what they all said! The bedroom however, was still very much that of a young boy's – dispersed amongst carelessly flung clothes were illustrations of Rhen's secluded interests; monster figurines scattered on the floor, posters advertising vampires and deep-sea creatures coating the sandstone brick walls. Rheneas had never been to the pictures, but Balfour had an older friend whose uncle collected film memorabilia and happily shared it with him. Balfour never cared for that stuff – he was always the one dragging his little brother outside because they were one short of a rugby team. Until Rhen was old enough to buy himself a train ticket to the big city, he'd have to live out his science fiction fancies through books alone.

Ah who cares. The flicks are just the same as books, only moving and talking. Don't use your brain proper. At times it was easier to pretend he wasn't interested in fascinating new technologies like film production. Rheneas picked up his deflated football (there'd been nobody to play with since his brother disappeared) and slumped onto the bed with his back to the wall, feeling the stonework cling to his wool pullover and grasping strands of his hair with a wonderful static electricity. The Hammerheads logo on the face of his old football was faded and warped from years of mud-caked tackles and torpedo kicks to the belly.

It's the old logo anyway, he thought, ditching the ball at the opposite wall and watching in amusement as it rolled back towards him.

It's on purpose, Balfour used to say, *they make a new logo every few seasons so you have to buy the new merch!*

In his naivety Rheneas could not believe his beloved rugby team would trick him into doing such a thing, but *it's business* – Balfour would chirp, and Rheneas hated him for trying to be smart. He threw the ball at the wall again and cursed at the sound it made – he'd have to be quieter lest he incited his mother's grief again. As for the grubby marks the ball left on the wall – nothing a new movie poster wouldn't cover up.

Rheneas was about to resign himself to an early night's sleep when an object flew through the open window and landed lightly on the floor next to the bed. It was a piece of paper scrunched into a ball, and it startled him more than he'd ever admit to anybody. Instead of inspecting the paper he dashed to the window and saw a raincoated figure hurrying away through the downpour.

Weird.

The paper was damp on the exterior but thankfully the pen strokes within had not run too much. Rheneas read,

Cousin of mine told me about a shaman in the village ruins – few clicks north of here. Knows about the Wights. Might know about Balfour? Let's check it out. Hope you're ok. – Pidgee.

Clairvoyance

She was so sick of green. It was everywhere; green, green, green. In that ocean of trees, green. In the night skies decorated with cloud, green. Even her namesake – Lucida Green! The word and its very definition had lost all meaning to her. Many a day would pass where she would see nothing of the spectrum other than those dirty and cool tones; the brown of earth, the blue of sky and the green of tree; green that had begun to dirty the palette and seep into the other tones. Where was violet and its royal opulence? Or the red of blood – the only red she ever saw these days was the crest of the Knock Tern named Nettles. In he would swoop at any time he pleased, never with anything important to divulge, rather reappearing to confirm that young Lucida still tailed along with him. There were other birds too; the Halcyon Kookas laughed constantly, mocking her dehydration with phony proclamations of impending rain. Lucida was sweating less as time went on, and she knew this was a very bad thing. She would have to find water soon; rain was far too temperamental, though it might have fallen at any moment, who could know its movements? Her dark skin was baked in the midday sun, black hair burning the scalp and luring the sun's ferocity towards her. It was these days that made her hate adventuring. Better to be at home, shaded from the day, crunching down on flavoured ice cubes her nanna used to make. But now wasn't the time to be maudlin. The wanderer was a figure of resilience, one who found home within themselves. *Spring followed winter*, soon she'd discover a town, another human being, *anything*. The gear amulet she had found took in the heat of the sun and seared her chest, inciting her anger, and she all at once stamped her dusty boots and took aim at a random gum tree.

"And why are you here? How are you unlike any other one of these, these, these *buggerful* trees?"

No answer – of course. This was a tree, after all, and a tree could not respond in a way she would understand.

"Why do you bother? Aren't you bored? It's all the same here!"

The tree stood its ground and mocked her with its silence.

"If I cut you down, some other tree would do your job – probably better than you!"

A light breeze ruffled the branches, and Nettles cawed in the distance. Lucida wiped her eye, thinking she'd clear away a tear, but her hand came back dry.

"I'm sorry I yelled at you."

What was wrong with her? Talking to trees, you're losing it now.

"Never mind."

The bushland had split itself in two, betwixt these two sandstone halves a valley ran. Lucida ran her eye over the high cliff face on her left; stunted eucalypt grew out the side of the wall, and under their shallow roots she could discern the eroded patterns where water long gone had carved its sigil in waves. She was too late to drink of that flow, too late by millennia. Still, where valleys ran, water often did so as well, and Lord knew Lucida did not have the energy to summit the cliff faces either side of her. The valley was thick with undergrowth, their deeper greens teasing her with thoughts of water, and indeed their verdancy belayed to the presence of it nearby. She could almost smell the creek that eluded her. She hacked at swathes of foliage with her machete and listened intently for Nettles to cry out and alert her of wonderful discovery. Bursting into a clearing Lucida saw Nettles, perched not by the shore of some river but at the apex of a dingy shack of corrugated iron, posed with wing tucked up like some rusty weathervane.

"What's here, Nettles?"

Lucida peered into the window of the shack and behind the razor-sharp broken glass saw nothing but darkness and shadows. It was a furnished home, and seemed too orderly to be unoccupied. The layout of its construction was poorly designed, for the shack consisted of a single room flanked on opposite walls by two doors, so that the wind would race straight through if it happened to blow in that particular direction. Not that it would take much to knock it down anyway, for Lucida observed the rotted wooden pillars that propped the whole place up warp beneath the weight of heated iron sheets. There was a small table, sheets of curtain or some other material and many little trinkets of forgotten origin. But the wandering girl saw past all of this and out the other side of the shack; there framed by the second doorway was a bubbling spring back against the sandstone cliff. Fearing a trap, she raced around the shack instead of through it and, unable to restrain her thirst, drove her face into the cool puddle of water and slurped greedily. Like an animal she guzzled, blinded by the euphoria of a drought broken and unaware of the squalid woman who had emerged from inside the shack.

"Drinkin' from me private spring, is it?"

Lucida started; from her knelt position the woman towered over her menacingly (though Lucida would be much taller than her when she stood). She was a shrivelled old thing – a face like a sun-dried tomato and a smell like one left soured in the heat. From her head a platted braid swung hypnotically, and Lucida saw she had little hair other than this. How ancient this woman might be, Lucida could not guess.

"And I suppose she's hungry too..."

Lucida cleared her throat, "If it please, just the water is fine,"

The old woman laughed, "She's got manners! That is unusual..."

In truth, Lucida was starving but didn't care to press her luck with this woman. For all she knew she'd be fed poison, or fattened up and eaten – she'd read her share of faery tales. But to spin it another way, give the tale another ending – possibility came to Lucida. If this woman tried anything, she reckoned she could take her down easily. To pummel an old lady; never a pleasant thought in any case, but Lucida hoped it would not come to this. All the while the hag eyed her up and down, jealous of banished youth and vengeful to Father Time who stole it.

"Two," the old woman croaked, "Two visitors I've had in the past moon. None for a good decade, now two. And what do they call you?"

Lucida stood and gave her best curtsy, though doing so she looked little more than a stilted flamingo in such begrimed boots and pants, "I am Lucida."

"A bright one. I am Ellameno Pea."

"Is that a joke?"

Ellameno burst out laughing as though it was, "Haw! 'Spose ye might say so. Frankly they's the only letters I knowed."

"Wait – you spell it 'LMNOP'? How about just Ella? Or Miss Pea, perhaps?"

"Means nothing to me."

"Well, nice to meet you," but there was great hesitancy in her voice. The old woman looked ready to curl over and die; would she stay standing if Lucida puffed a breath in her direction? A purple sack covered her entire form and gave her the appearance of a misshapen eggplant, and Lucida realised that this sack had been the very same curtain-like material she'd observed inside the shack. Miss Pea must have been sitting there the whole time watching her. A crooked stick with a few brown gum leaves rustled as she waved it, pointed at Nettles who had perched on Lucida's shoulder and concealed his face.

"That's a pretty bird," said Pea, "Been too long since I've had knock tern."

Lucida gave her a sideways glance, "Yes. He's well trained, too. Can tear an eye out before it can blink."

A guttural chuckle escaped the old woman's dusty lips; Lucida took note of a small skull pinned at her collar – probably a lizard or a small bird. Nettles was clearly uncomfortable in her presence, giving off that animal wariness that humans often failed to read.

"I thank you for the drink," said Lucida, "and would ask that I might fill my decanter and be on my way."

"In such a hurry to leave, is she? She wandered so long without finding anybody and now she wants to be alone again already."

The wandering girl gave a start, "How did you know that?"

Pea laughed again, "I could claim it clairvoyance but nay, this be because I know there ain't nobody for many miles. Unless ye saw the young boy who passed through my grounds earlier, there's nobody else here to see."

Lucida knew she was being drawn in by the woman's sycophant claims, but could not help but probe her for more information. After all, she'd yearned for human company so long, surely this unpleasant woman could at least inform her of the correct direction to wander.

"Young boy?"

"Come sit," replied Pea, "I make ye some tea."

To Lucida it would seem that time had sunk into a formless void, for she found herself camped beneath a sunset sky around a crude fire her strange host had provided. Given how late the sun set in those parts, she knew it was indeed getting late, and somehow the old hag had held her attention for such an amount of time. Ellameno had served up a dirty-coloured brew she affectionately referred to as bush tea; Lucida kept a keen eye on its construction, watched for the old hag to drink of it first to confirm it was not poisoned. After that it was a simple matter of fishing the bugs out of those tin cups and it was almost a tolerable beverage. It was the first truly flavourful morsel Lucida had consumed in a long while, and the bland taste of the bushland's offerings was soon forgotten. The fire dwindled, and the young girl kept expecting the hag to point her stick at the ashes and re-ignite them but no, this was an ordinary old woman – a little crazed, but surely just that.

"Long time gone since I seen another person," muttered Ellameno Pea, "so fancy me surprise when two children pass through in the space of a week."

"Would I know this boy?"

Lucida realised it was a stupid question. She knew very few from Calumnia and even if she did know of this lad, why would the old lady know this too? Old habits died hard, it would seem, and Lucida still had a small inclination that this woman might be psychic.

"Roughed up thing, he was. Maybe a tad younger than yourself – only the first signs of peach fuzz on his face. Came a'wandering through me grounds and wouldn't share a word. Stared right through when I tried to speak with him. Young ones these days, the rudeness..."

"He didn't say anything?"

"A few scattered words, nothing c'herent if you please," continued Pea, "was looking for a place in the pines, was asking for his brother."

"Drop a name?"

"Was getting to that – Wood note. Kept saying it. A name, maybe? I don't know."

"Weird."

"Yes, weird; but these days are stranger than most, I've lived to see a couple, ha! But ye must tell of your story. Pretty thing like you shouldn't be living the wanderer's life. 'Tis thankless, I says."

Lucida never liked to be called pretty – the word sounded small and pathetic to her, and when uttered by an ugly old geriatric she felt somewhat repulsed. Still, her manners stayed with her, and for most part they never steered her wrong.

"Nanny's old," Lucida said, "Who knows how long she'll last. And there I was crammed up in some boarding school. So I decided I'd go find Nanny instead; better to be at her side than stuck at some snooty school."

There was little else she could say without choking up, although the pangs of loneliness would ebb and flow, it still pained Lucida to recall her grandmother for too long.

Big girls didn't cry, either. Pretty ones might, but tough ones didn't.

"So it's the travelling bug, aye. She's a fickle and furious itch," said Pea, "and ne'er you fret about yer nanny; when you're as old as me losing people becomes second nature and ye count the days until it's yerself that's a leaving."

"What a horrible thing to say."

"Ha! I don't dance 'round the shit no more, sweet girl. Discretion vacates a person with each new wrinkle, eh he."

"And how many moons might you've seen, ma'am?"

Ellameno Pea took on a grave expression, a look so empty that one might very well travel along the river of ages in those milky eyes, "Eh, enough to remember some stuff no-one else would. How the world used to be before – ah never mind. Too much for yer ripe young brain."

Lucida drained her cup and tried to look impressive in doing so, "I'd hear it if you care."

"Nay, nay. Not nice to dwell on the old ways – take that as advice, missy. Will make the sting o' death less potent on yer heart." On a sudden she became tearfully desperate, "Will ye stay a night at least? Ye see I'm alone so much."

The old hag looked powerless in that moribund state; shoulders slouched with the defeat of years, yearning earnestly for human contact. A kind heart had always been stitched in Lucida's psyche, and she hated to upset an elderly woman so, but she had to move on – it was the way of the wanderer. She looked east and saw the dawn-lit sky slowly increase in pallor.

"Perhaps another hour or so – then I must be off."

"I can make more tea, share a fortune – would you like to hear yer final words? 'Tis an old carnival trick o' mine."

"No, please understand."

"Alright, alright," Pea shrugged, "stubborn lot you youths."

"If you could just tell me where I might find the next town..."

Pea smirked, "Well I assumes you've come from Calumnia; very mention of *snooty boarding school* reminds me o' that place. Nearest town? Why it ain't far for those young legs. Same way the boy went. Day or two hiking, and far enough away from where ye've escaped."

With no more than a point of a crooked finger in the northerly direction Lucida was prepped to push on her way. Nettles returned with the sunrise, having not wanted to spend any further time with the old woman than necessary. For Ellameno Pea, she looked on Lucida's leaving with an almost motherly longing, perhaps the first kindling of a compassionate fire she'd felt in decades. Still Lucida refused to get too close, although later she would feel bad for not trusting the lady a little more. But those feelings would remain abated while she stewed on Pea's parting words,

"What yer lookin' for – hope yer more fruitful than they was."

The Disclaimer

The cabinet meeting room could be likened to a courtroom and library hybrid; a great mahogany chair headed the back wall, below a gallantly decorated shield depicting the *Gull and Leviathan*. Beneath this great chair and lectern was a hemispherical run of wooden benches, punctuated into segments by little green lamp and desk pairings – not unlike a school auditorium (and pity be with any left-handed patrons, for the desks were exclusively for their more common opposite. Lady Libra was, in fact, *gauche* in dexterity, but that was only a minor detail). The centre of this auditorium was reserved for a long wooden table lined on either side with a row of wooden chairs, whereupon the two competing political parties would place their 'front-liners' as it were.

At present only one side of this table was occupied – that of the opposition leader Austin Spindle and his assistant Silas. A dull murmur perpetuated through the echoed chamber, of mutterings betwixt party members on the wooden benches and the Adjudicator – who sat atop the throne-like chair in the middle – humming to himself and cleaning his nails. Spindle shifted uncomfortably in his seat, rapping his sullen knuckles on the bench before him in an empty percussion. And each time he shifted, a blunt thud was heard, followed by a series of unintelligible curses, for Spindle's legs were rather too long for such rigid seatings and he crashed his knees against the table with each movement. For Silas, there was no such issue, for there was unfortunately no feeling in his legs, but he nonetheless found himself flustered as Spindle edged this way and that for comfort, wishing he could just glue the man's posterior to the chair so he would cease fidgeting.

"Well then," hissed Spindle, "Two minutes past the hour of ten. Where is our opposition?"

The Adjudicator, a perfunctory old vulture to be sure, did not look up from his lectern and drawled slowly, "Miss Tenebrific will be a few minutes, Mr. Spindle; she is usually late."

"And? This is our expectation for the one who runs the entirety of Verdigris?" Spindle chuckled, but when he looked around at his fellow party members, he saw that none of them shared in the joviality. Whether they had not listened to him or simply didn't find the humour in their leader's remark was up for debate.

"Clearly she does not respect the busyness of our great party!" Spindle chuffed.

A heavy thump resonated through the chamber, and Spindle realised one of his members had dozed off and fallen head first onto the desk at which he sat.

"Herm, that is to say," - (a loud snoring now sounded) - "that we are..." he trailed off, but with nobody really listening, the fact that he did not finish his sentence was of no matter.

The doors of the auditorium presently flung open, and there in all her weighted grandeur was the Lady Libra Tenebrific. Eclipsed behind her planet-like dimensions her party members trailed in, headed by the young lady Polly Jean Cupio, like the tail of some mighty meteor. Again, without raising his head, the Adjudicator bellowed forth, "Our respected leader, Miss Tenebrific and party. Do we have your blessing to begin?"

The Lady Libra threw her hand as if to say *very well* as the party members took their seats. Amongst the scuffling there was another bang and another curse as Spindle knocked his knee once more on the table in front of him. Miss Libra, on the other hand, had troubles of a different kind. Pursing her lips, she warily eyed the wooden chair on which she was to ensconce, before attempting to lower her enormous bulk into it. There sounded a creaking as Libra's hips pressed on the armrests of her chair; she shifted herself by degrees into the seat, great pillows of flesh bulging over the armrests like rising sea foam as she struggled. She huffed uncomfortably as a stifling pain shot through her sides, but she was seated, at last, and discomfort aside, was ready to proceed.

I could swear these chairs are getting smaller…

When the Adjudicator finally looked up it was plain to see he was in no mood to be in the windowless meeting room; his eyes were rheumy behind his spectacles as he stroked at his long moustache. *Too many decades have been wasted here,* he mused, *and meanwhile my grandchildren play in the sun. Oh, to be young again.*

"We bring these issues to the attention of the parties," he sighed, "The voting public have shown chief concern on the safety of jobs in line with the price of goods and services -"

"My good Adjudicator," Spindle interjected, "surely you've not forgotten the refreshments!"

A collective sigh echoed through the chambers, one of both disgust and relief; the Adjudicator, in no mood to be there any longer than need be, rolled his eyes impatiently at the interruption. For Spindle, and really everybody else, it was some reprieve to at least enjoy a hot coffee while dealing with such tedious matters. Polly Jean, who'd unwillingly taken on the role of waitress at these meetings, wheeled a tea tray next to Miss Libra (God forbid if she wasn't served first), and poured from a great urn with precarious dexterity. A hearty selection of biscuits was placed in generous amounts onto Libra's plate with little silver tongs – so much so that there were no treats left for young Silas when Polly Jean had reached him. Seemingly disappointed to have been robbed of one hedonistic vice in the otherwise flagellating meeting, Silas dropped his shoulders. But when his plate was placed before him, he smiled and saw an exquisite tart placed upon it. Polly Jean smiled sweetly at him – a smile that betrayed her shyness and self-reservation but could so easily be taken for flirtatious. In spite of the lack of blood flow to certain regions of his person, Silas was still a hot-blooded young man who unfortunately took Polly's look to be the latter mentioned, and for the rest of the meeting found himself stealing not-so-discreet glances at the pretty young lady who acted as Libra's servant. In a rather surprising gesture, Spindle agreed to an intensely flavoured brew that was the utter opposite to the tepid swill he would procure in his own home. A surprising gesture that is, until one realised that it was not Spindle who paid for the refreshments offered in parliament, and that his effortless grasp at a free beverage made him all the more prudish.

Polly wheeled the tea tray towards the adjudicator, "Sir?"

"Ah, no thank you miss," came his reply. It was the principle of it all – to accept anything from her would be hypocritical to his stance on the selfish nature of the government. Later though, he wished he had agreed to even a small sample; his stomach growled as he espied Libra stuffing yet another pastry past her lips, and upon the realisation that lunch was still several hours away.

"Would the Incumbent care to respond first?"

"Do not call me that," Libra drawled, "as though I were something to be cast aside so easily."

"I doubt she could be shifted swiftly…" muttered Silas, to which Polly Jean tittered.

The meeting descended into a cesspool of disclaimers in which neither party would claim truth or falsity in anything. It was about saying the right thing, after all, and covering one's self from any absurdity that might be misconstrued from cherry-picked sentences.

"The opinions I express are those of my party!" cried Spindle.

"Sir?" replied the Adjudicator, "I'm afraid you cannot claim that."

….

"I always tell the truth, that is the only true lie."

….

"The public will like what I like. The public like me."

….

"The public will hate me and like what I do."

….

"All opinions are mine own, unless they are wrong."

….

"Everything you say and do will reflect upon your entire party. That is unless it is a bad or distasteful thing in which the blame rests entirely on the public eye for jumping to conclusions."

….

"The Incumbent speaks with her mouth full!"

….

The stenographer (who in this case was a dwarfish woman whose fingers were far too stubby to type smoothly) could barely keep up as the barrage of outrageous claims and backhanded insults flew across both sides of the room. Libra and Spindle, commanders of their own bootlicking battalions, had aimed the crosshairs of their taunts directly at one another.

"You've little to show by way of servitude to any bar yourself!" cried Spindle.

"And what exactly have you done?" sighed Libra, "You're as expendable as the rest."

"You would suggest myself a throttlebottom?" Spindle fumed.

Polly Jean burst with a snigger and hurriedly wiped the spittle from her chin.

"What's funny, Miss Cupio?"

"Oh, ignore the girl, Spindle," said Libra, "you've more important foes at hand."

"Devalued by her very superior! Objection!"

"This isn't a courthouse, Mr. Spindle." The Adjudicator droned.

"Then I will have the floor! Or whatever it is I'm supposed to say."

"Very well then."

"I… I… D'oh I lost my train of thought! You see what this woman does to me?"

"I am merely sitting here, Spindle. Sitting here watching you implode," said Libra.

"My point… That is to say, my *raison d'etre* is for the *noblisse oblige!*" puffed Spindle.

"Use as many big words as you please, it does not make the man any bigger,"

"Oh, you sneaky! What I say is we must live by example here! The people can't expect us to lap up luxury while they suffer!"

"What's that?" yawned Libra, "Why I think you bored me to sleep there for a second. I'd no idea that was actually possible…"

From one corner, Silas stared at Polly Jean, who in turn stared fawningly at Libra, whose cutting glare sent an involuntary shudder down Spindle's spine. The Adjudicator removed a pocket watch from his gowns and raised it to one inch of distance from his left eye.

"Ah yes, good talk, everyone. We'll adjourn here."

Austin Spindle was abashed and stammered, "We'll what? Impossible! We've barely started!"

But the masses were already filing out of the meeting room like school-children dismissed for recess. Silas wheeled his chair over to Polly Jean and made a feeble attempt to assist her with her coat. But given the height difference enforced by his permanent recline, Miss Cupio came close to stumbling over several times. Her demeanour was too polite to reject this act of chivalry, yet like most kindly folk who are averse to displeasing people but dislike attention, she came across as brash and rude to young Silas, shooting him a shy smile before attending to cavalry of coffee cups left behind by the politicians. For Silas, his heart pounded with affection; in a matter of minutes he had decided that this stunning creature who served under Lady Libra deserved every ounce of doting capable to him. He simply must speak to her!

But here? Impossible!

His heart continued to thunder spasmodically; he was easily startled when Austin Spindle slammed his knee into the table yet again, sending shockwaves through the coffee cups that Polly Jean had moved so swiftly to detain. The storm of exiting people slowly subsided, and Lady Libra, who (due to the immensity of her personality) was normally the forefront of any grand commotion, was in fact the last one left in the meeting room. She discreetly shifted this way and that, before tapping her foot impatiently. It would seem that she was waiting for everyone else to leave, but Polly Jean took notice of her (such was her vocation) and softly spoke, "Miss, will you be leaving too?"

Lady Libra was flushed red in the face and cleared her throat, "I, uh, will need to attend to this paperwork first. That will be all, Miss Cupio."

"Oh, ok," Polly tittered, "but should I…"

"Go, Polly."

"Yes, miss!"

The door slammed shut and all was silent, save for the receding patter of Polly Jean's timorous gait.

Had she noticed?

Libra felt the burning embarrassment rush over her as she placed her hands on the armrests of her chair. She grunted and tried to wedge herself out but she was stuck fast.

Those who toil shall be lifted indeed! thought Libra, *I will need to have a word with our interior decorators about this furniture…*

Polly & Silas

The great clock tower that loomed over the central business district belted out the sixth hour bell. Across the icy cobblestones weary business men and women walked with an exhausted vigour, for the evening had arrived, and with it came the promise of warm homes and rest. Steam spewed into the starry sky as the trams trundled along their steel rails, hanging about the air in vapours not unlike the breath of the pedestrians who nuzzled their chins into their scarves and stuffed their hands into their coat pockets. Magna Luxuria was dressed in a most beautiful twilit glow, as the sky washed away from an apricot gold into a navy night dotted with starlight. On *terra firma*, other stars twinkled – that of snowflakes reflected in streetlamps, covering untrodden places with frigid diamonds. The smell of burning coal was overpowering as chimney stacks belched their wastrel smoke into the otherwise pure air of Cardinal Mons, and the evening travellers each hurried onto their respective trains.

How beautiful the sight of industry turning in for the night, having earned a restful fruit from their days labour; in our minds' eyes the crowds part and our focus narrows in on two particular individuals whom we recognise as Polly Jean Cupio and Silas Krummholz, the chief assistants of the opposing leaders Tenebrific and Spindle. Both had toiled greatly that day, perhaps more so than most, yet neither were to be lifted, as their home city's mighty motto would claim. Now, usually there would be no chance of these two crossing paths on their commute home from the Governing House (for Polly Jean lived with her parents in a humble apartment in the suburbs of Magna Austrinus, whilst Silas took roost on the opposite reaches of town in Magna Austere), but tonight was different for the simple fact that Silas was following the young girl who'd so sweetly smiled at him in the morning cabinet meeting. And before the reader leaps to outrageous conclusions of ill-intent, we are reminded of the gentle nature of Silas, his somewhat nervous disposition and of course, his non-threatening stature of being wheelchair-bound. No, Silas merely wished to speak with Polly Jean, but his anxious demeanour was holding him back to such ridiculous extent that it would seem to any onlooker that he was stalking the poor girl.

Polly had not noticed him as she bustled onto the trolley at the central station and taken her seat between a rather smelly woman and sweaty old man. Buried as she was in the pleasures of a novel, she did not observe Silas awkwardly hoist himself onto the same carriage and wheel his way to the space reserved for people with his predicament. And he could get no closer to Polly, which only heightened his shyness and made his face flush red with humiliation.

At what point is this considered stalking? Does it count as stalking if I actually speak to her?

Polly stirred at the sound of a commotion at the front of the trolley; a portly woman had become unbalanced by a jolt in the tracks and had spilled her thermos on the shoes of poor Silas. The young man hissed as the hot tea scalded through his socks but did his best not to shout any profanity in the presence of others, especially she who he was trying to impress. The innumerable apologies of the thermos lady were hardly heard by Silas, who realised Polly had noticed him at last.

Not the ideal way to get attention, but it worked....

His face went redder than ever; the thermos lady fawned on Silas, as he found people often did. He could not help but feel that he was pitied, and that for this able-legged woman to spill tea on him, well – she may as well have murdered a nun! Desperately he implored the lady that it was ok; the commotion frustrated him greatly. Polly smiled awkwardly at nobody in particular before returning to the pages of her book.

Is that the man from today? Of course, what other wheelchair-bound men have you met today? I should go sit with him, for he certainly can't amble on up here. Oh, Polly don't be rude! Besides, I don't know him well enough – I should just pretend I haven't noticed him.

Silas, who had hoped that the commotion with the spilt tea would garner Polly's interest, was heartily disappointed to see her return to her reading. He fidgeted about – tapping his fingers on his knees and puffing out his breath with exasperation.

She didn't see. Or didn't recognise me. Or did *recognise me and is ignoring me. Oh, my wretched heart! Have I seen her before? I must have, standing in Miss Tenebrific's shadow no doubt. But now that darkness has lifted – she's beautiful – and I just may have had any dignified chance of speaking to her stolen by some foolish woman with an unsteady hand!*

The tea that splashed his legs had gone tepid; his shoes would be stained. Dusk had given way to night as the train continued along its way, Silas saw buildings he had never seen before, and as for those places he *had* seen – they were far off in the distance, and looked so different from the angle he now saw them. He had not been to this side of the city for many years.

Well I must speak to her now – it would at least give some reason to my gallivanting off to the other side of town. Hopefully she alights at a busy place – lest I look even more suspicious.

She didn't. Polly Jean's tram stop was a dingy old corner bereft of any charm and scarred by the blemishes of soot and charcoal. Such was the maladroit geometry of the buildings around her that the wind scarcely found passage through these streets, and the filth of old ashen snowfall and of dumped fireplace cinders remained on the putrid cobblestones for weeks at a time. Lord knew the street-sweepers had more opulent boulevards to keep clean. Silas watched Polly exit the tram and decided to alight himself at the next stop, just down the road from her. That way it may not have looked quite so obvious that she was the object of his current venture, and hopefully he could catch up to her in good enough time. Ignoring the final apology from the tea lady, he was swiftly able to maneuverer himself off the trolley and onto the street, where more apologies were uttered, this time from other pedestrians who got in his way as he eagerly wheeled in the direction of Polly's alighting. The crowds dissipated slowly as she came into view. Keeping Polly at a suitable distance was no issue for Silas; the few people that were around continued to keep his path clear due to the simple fact that he was crippled. To him, it was so utterly condescending – pedestrians giving him a wide berth on the footpaths out of what they would deem curtesy. But their sidelong glances and mutterings reeked of awkward avoidance, as if they could catch paraplegia like a common cold. Recent technological advancements had seen automaton legs produced for people in his position, but Silas thought them somewhat undignified. Given the steepness of the Magna Austrinus hills, he found himself wishing for a pair of those pistons if only for that moment. He charged on uphill, observing Polly making a left turn into a quieter laneway. The lithe muscles of Silas' arms ached with exertion, and the sweat that formed in his armpits out of nerves as much as exercise turned clammy in the cold evening. Rounding the corner himself he was relieved at the further reduction in crowd, yet sighed longingly to see yet another incline between himself and Polly, who had reached the top of the hill to the frontage of the home she shared with her parents. The turn of a key and the clack of a closing door and she was gone, and so too went any purpose behind Silas' little sojourn across town.

Real bright, Silas. What are you doing here? Oh well, at least I won't have to climb that hill.

The light of the ante-room was dull, yet its lustre was still enough to chase off the demons of the dark that lurked in Polly's ashy street. Her heart thudded violently as she removed her coat and scarf and kicked her shoes to the corner. The sounds of her homestead descended – the clattering of pots in the kitchen and the prattling voices of her father's new television set (were it not crass to say, he would call it his pride and joy – but customs deemed it better he called his only daughter his pride and joy, not that Polly cared). Polly's ears burned hotly, although her feet were cold; her armpits sweated awfully but her spine tingled with a shiver. It was a modest home, at least by the standard of Cardinal Mons. She had lived here her entire life, always too timid to venture beyond her parents' world, and indeed her timidity frustrated her greatly, for her parents were impossibly irritating, and it would be of little doubt to any observer that they held her back from greatness with the invisible chains of self-doubt lashed about many children of any age. The automation of the evening settled on the triptych – food was partaken in front of the television, where all three of them faced that magic box like moths to a blue lamp, moths that rarely glanced at each other as they shook the clotted dust of the day from their ragged wings.

"It would be nice if you were home a little earlier, sweetheart,"

"Yes, mother," Polly's eyes looked through the television, focused on the knitted picture of a bushland river that hung on the wall behind it. She'd often drift into that world of ochre-coloured yarn; television was of little interest to her; God forbid her father looked up from the screen long enough to notice. She knew her mother was looking at her, and felt a small chip of herself rust away with each glance.

"I won't be here forever, you know. Who'll cook you dinner when I'm gone? Will you just eat at an ungodly late hour each night? Oh, the strains you put your poor mother under!"

"Yes, mother,"

Polly's mother continued to eye off her daughter, "Eat! You're so thin! You know, sweetheart, I really think you could do more to entice a nice man,"

"Yes, mother,"

"What, eat too much and she'll be too fat to wed!" chortled her father, "Pol, you see the rich suitors tying themselves to the heavyset girls?"

"No, father,"

"Literal anchor there, my girl,"

"Well it's no excuse to refuse the roast I slaved over. Eat!"

"Yes, mother,"

"It's that job of yours, Pol; to think, a woman working such hours! Pah! And I suppose you'll be wanting Tenebrific's job next?

"Not really, father,"

"Don't pressure the poor girl, you lout! How will she run a home and a country at the same time! Here, sweetheart, you haven't touched your potatoes,"

"Yes, mother,"

"Apples and oranges, wife! Comparing the running of our great country to one house on the hill? Pol, are you hearing this?"

"Yes, father,"

"The nerve! Oh, my heart could bleed so! Your dessert is ready, just as it has been every night for twenty years! And who would make it otherwise? Oh, I ought to kick the stool out. I'll do it one day, and that will certainly show you! Sweetheart, I'll give you extra pie – your ungrateful father has squandered his privilege much as my life was when I married him! Oh, the years gone!"

"Yes, mother,"

"And for what? I won't even see a grandchild at this rate!"

"Damn it, woman!" at last his eyes were wrestled away from the television screen, "I earn my feed for this family! You want grandchildren? Quit giving her so much food! I hear too much sugar stunts yer fertility,"

"Please don't talk about my 'fertility', father,"

"Eh?"

"Never mind.... Mother, thank you for dinner. I'm tired,"

If her mother had heard her give thanks, she certainly didn't show it, and they bickered more as Polly climbed her narrow steps up to the second floor, where two bedrooms and a bathroom pressed together in impossibly small confines. There was barely any room to move on that second floor, and Polly had always hated how the steep stairs groaned under the slightest weight, making her feel a thousand times heavier than she was in actuality.

"Listen to those steps," came her mother's voice (was it a reality or was she only recalling a past comment?), "so heavyset! Oh, she'll never find anybody!"

Polly wondered why, in fact, she *needed* to find anybody. She didn't know what to think of herself, but to her it didn't matter what she thought – it never had, and seemed like it never would. Her bedroom was a low-ceilinged box with walls that had yellowed with age; this off-coloured light made her aching head swim, the pressure behind her eyes was always so intense at the end of a work day. She sat in her low chair and leant her arm on the cold window sill. Silence pervaded; Polly thought of the woman who ordered her around each day at work and felt a fluttering in her stomach that was both disconcerting and comforting at the same time. Her ears rang with the absence of sound and she felt a looseness in her gut – she could never tell if this was anxiety or pleasure. In any account, her eyes dilated as she sat dazed, completely one with her bedroom, knowing any movement now would probably break the spell she was under.

My feet aren't so big, she thought, *but it isn't the size is it? Mum's always banging on about stomping. Don't stomp, Pol! Maybe that's just the sound my feet make.*

There was a sound at the window, or at least she thought she heard one, and she stood. No, no sound, but here the spell hadn't broken yet.

I feel so stuffed – how is Libra able to eat so much?

Was it that she *wanted* Libra, or to *be* Libra? Polly didn't quite understand her own feelings. What was it about Libra? To many she was repulsive, yet there was something in her confidence - that bloated, overt confidence that drew Polly towards her. That aura of a siren drifting outwards from her divine orbit, her gravity pulling any whim towards her like an anchor chain hauled from the sea.

She was stuck in that chair, I know it. But that won't change her.

She remembered the one time as a child when she'd visited the seaside near Banksia. The seagulls would converge on the boardwalks and eat whatever scraps came their way. They'd eat as if there was no tomorrow, even to excess, even to the point of being too heavy and bloated to fly away – and then the stray cats would... Polly snatched up the feather boa from her dresser and tucked it about her shoulders; it was a tacky old thing, fuchsia in colour and worn with age – she had had it since she was a child. Tossing her hair over her shoulder, Polly looked down her nose at mirror above the dresser. She shoved her hands onto her hips and tried her best authoritative stance and....

This doesn't work.

Too skinny, she thought, *there's no power in my appearance. I just look like an insect.*

Polly tried to push her belly out as far as she could, but this accomplished little more than a minor distension in her svelte frame, so she instead slumped onto the seat before her dresser and lay with her head down on the table top.

Might just sleep here.... No don't be stupid.

She dimmed the lights and slouched into bed, willing the darkness and covers to conceal her completely. Closing her eyes, she brought to mind the aroma of Libra's perfume, and hoped she could cling to that thought until sleep took her.

It was ten o'clock by the time Silas returned home. His flat was situated up a single flight of stairs, and despite the difficulty it presented each day, he knew how to laboriously drag himself and his chair up the steps one by one. The evening held a piqued fatigue for him; what a waste of time, chasing that girl around town. And to think he didn't even muster the courage to speak to her! The single room of his flat greeted him with indifference; it was cold, and having been unattended to all day, it would take some time to heat.

Better to just bury myself in blankets...

Removing his glasses, he winced at the pinched pain on the bridge of his nose. Damned things, his glasses were – he'd never been fond of wearing them.

Just one more function cruel nature decided to deprive me of – well we are dramatic this evening, Silas...

To do something enjoyable – that was the tonic. A nice cup of tea, perhaps. Sure, it was late, and work would start at the same early hour the next day, but at that moment Silas was able to embrace his isolation and breathe a sigh of relief. With yet another exerted effort he removed his clothes and, in spite of the cold, wheeled around in his underwear while the kettle boiled. There was not much in way of food for him that night, or any night for that matter, and Silas settled for a single piece of toast once again. His blurred reflection on the frosted window pane smeared a slouched and sombre figure. Silas curled his lip in disgust and flicked one of his nipples.

Hardly an Adonis now, am I? Well what can one expect of me. Bit hard to have a desirable physique in this condition.

His self-loathing had reached a climax; bottled all day and hidden behind faces of orderly conduct, it was only there in the loneliness of his flat that he could release, and being so tightly wound, it only took something small to throw him into a pitiful anger. His night shirt was tangled, he'd put it on inside out, and as he struggled to adjust it, the collar scratched irritably at his throat before he threw the damn thing on the floor.

"Argh fuck this thing!"

His rage left him as quickly as it had arrived. The kettle whistled, and outside the wind too, threw its own tune to the chorus. Silas breathed out and retrieved his night shirt. He looked back at the frosted window, this time looking past his reflection and trying to discern anything in the blackness of the night beyond. But there was nothing to see. He wondered if anybody in the world thought of him at the end of each day.

The Fourth Reflection

Impatiently, with a mind stuffed full of loud and interrupting thoughts, Lewiston stood with feet apart. The tiled wall inches from his face might have been these very thoughts ironed out in perfect little white squares, all of identical shape and size in orderly pattern upon the wall; yet to stare at them too long was to become muddled and overwhelmed. In their plainness they were busy, vying for attention yet offering nothing of extravagance. Lewiston puffed his cheeks; there was an aching in his loins that just wasn't letting up.

"A man of science, meets his older colleague; maybe an old teacher? And..."

The piss wasn't coming. Exasperated, Lewiston exhaled and squeezed his eyes shut.

"Relax. Won't happen if you think too much. An older friend with a superstition. The young man finds it ridiculous."

The dull thud of the bathroom door opening shocked him more than it should have. The voice that followed echoed indifferently - some bloke on his phone. He stood next to Lewiston at the urinal, effortlessly whipped his member out and pissed freely, the phone wedged between ear and shoulder,

"Yep. Yep, the grey nut. No, the grey one. Turn that. Not there, the one next to the wheel arch? Under there, yeah, a metal slot. Little metal slot."

Any hope Lewiston had of relieving himself dissipated as this stranger's voice added its song to his crippled mind. The other man was done; he left in a hurry (washing his hands had evidently never entered his mind) and Lewiston sobbed inwardly and tried to start the process again. He knew it shouldn't be this difficult, but he'd always been the type to overcomplicate matters, even those of a biological function. Whether it was fulfilling a natural urge or attempting to piece together a new story, Lewiston always had to do it the hard way. For a moment his mind flatlined completely - too much going on, like several people trying to fit through a door simultaneously - but then, then,

"Oh thank fuck," he whispered.

The hot liquid streamed out of him, and the shocking smell of ammonia knocked a bit more sense into him.

"Tetraphobia." He thought, "fear of the number 4."

It was a ludicrous concept to Lewiston, but he'd thought he could write an interesting story about it.

"And the old teacher warns the young man not to be cynical and -"

The last trickle of his water spattered onto his shoe, and Lewiston cursed again. At this rate he'd never get this story off the ground. It was always difficult to be creative on call. Deep down he regretted turning his hobby of literature into his profession. And with his overbearing wife... He glanced at his watch as he washed his hands.

"Fuck, gotta get home. Can't handle another of her blow ups."

For a moment he became self-conscious of the greying strands of hair that speckled his scalp and the slightest hint of a love handle poking out from the side of his waist, but now was not the time. The story had slipped again; it was almost as if it moved to a new location every time he blinked, and once he'd found it again, it would escape his grasp again. He left the toilets; the office was empty, its workers had all left, all bar Lewiston. He flicked the light switches and made his way to the elevator.

"Elevator pitch. Right, right, the story. Fear of four. Old man rambles about ancient oriental suspicion of that number, disruption of the Holy Trinity, what else?"

The elevator doors chimed and opened. Lewiston stepped inside.

"A blasphemous number and huh? Should I use 4?"

His jarred his finger pressing the button that would take him to the ground floor. He swore, sucked his injured digit then cursed himself for doing such a thing after touching a dirty elevator button.

"Maybe I'm too paranoid. 13. Some places don't have a 13th floor, right? Maybe I could use that."

The elevator shuddered and began its descent with Lewiston staring blankly at the mirrored wall of its interior. It was one of those infinite mirrors; a sheet of reflective glass on opposing walls to give the effect of multiple reflections extending into oblivion. The shoddy workmanship of the office building meant that these particular mirrors were not perfectly parallel, giving Lewiston a slightly curved train of images - his front, his back, his front, ad nauseum. He had always found this sort of optical illusion to be somewhat unsettling; the idea that the trick would carry on forever was too much for him to comprehend, like trying to understand the edge of the universe or the properties of time. Nonetheless he gazed at the striking sight absently as his elevator continued on with an augmented groaning.

On a sudden the groaning reached an abrupt crescendo, the elevator stopped in its tracks and Lewiston staggered to one knee. Silence pervaded. When he realised what had happened, his heart sunk - would that it could sink through the platform floor and carry him to freedom - but it was no good, the elevator had gotten stuck.

"Are you fucking kidding me?"

He cursed through his teeth and mashed the ground floor button with his fist; the lights flickered but little else. Lewiston couldn't believe his misfortune.

"Surely not. Come on, damn it I want to go home! What do you do here again? Right, the emergency button..."

Lewiston pressed the button, held it, smashed it, but nothing happened - the line was dead. He looked around the carriage for some means of escape - he had heard of plenty of different methods, but all of them in fictional tales. Trying the doors, he managed to get a finger hold between them but could not force them open any further. Above, a ventilation fan spun slowly but there was no sign of an access hatch of any kind. The fan blades rotated indifferently as Lewiston collected himself.

"Calm now, this ain't the end of the world. Someone will be alerted of this and fix it. Worse case is a night stuck here."

Would that be so bad? Time spent away from his overbearing wife sounded relieving - trapped in a steel box or not - and she could hardly blame him for this, could she? He muttered angrily to himself; she'd find a way to make it his fault - she always did - but that was a problem for another time.

Had anybody been alerted to his hitting of the emergency button? There had been no sign that it had done anything at all. Lewiston sighed and slumped to the floor; the pessimist in him said he wouldn't be found until his colleagues came to work the next morning.

How long had he sat there? He couldn't tell, and in his frazzled state he didn't think to check his watch. A sound of static crackled, and from the wall mounted speaker Lewiston heard a voice clear its throat. He leapt up and stepped towards the speaker as an unknown voice uttered, "Hello? Are you there?"

"Hello?! Yes, yes hello! The lift is stuck, I been here a while."

The voice was timorous, "a while?"

"Yes, a while, help me out here mate. What am I supposed to do?"

"Been there a while?"

"What? Yes, man!"

"Well I hardly see how that's your fault."

Lewiston winced in confusion.

"No... me neither. But can you help me?"

"I don't know."

"You don't know."

"No."

"What the f - whoever you are, guy, just help me!" *Who pays these blokes?*

There was silence for a moment before the timid voice replied, "I'll see."

Lewiston leaned closer to the speaker, "See what, exactly? How long do you think? Hello? Hello!"

The voice on the other end had disappeared; all that could be heard was the dull whir of the spinning ventilation fan. The fluorescent light flickered as Lewiston stood back up and sighed. He stared absently at his reflection before furrowing his brow - there was something wrong. The train of his reflection trailed off into infinity just as before, but there - one, two, three, four, the fifth reflection back - was an abnormality that could not possibly be correct. These types of mirrors were supposed to show his front and back in an alternating pattern, but there, fourth and fifth images down the trail, both reflections faced away from Lewiston. Optically this had to be impossible; he rubbed his eyes and looked again, only to see that the reflections had returned to their normal pattern.

"My head's broke, clearly." He muttered, "long day. I'm tired."

He continued to look, wondering if the illusion would appear again, but as he raised his finger to count the reflections, everything remained in order. But wait - no there was something wrong again; that fifth image of himself faced the right way but remained still when he raised his finger. He waved his arm, the crowd of reflections surrounding the fifth did as well, but that one reflection refused to conform. It - for he could hardly say he - stared at him with a smile that made him uncomfortable, and Lewiston thought himself to be hallucinating. What else could explain this?

A test, he thought to himself, *if only to appease my clearly overtired brain.*

He lowered himself into a crouch, so that he was below the level of the infinity mirror, before rising back to standing position. His heart jumped.

The fourth reflection was missing.

Lewiston felt his heart rate rising. A simple blink of the eyes and everything was back to normal.

"This is ridiculous." He pressed the emergency button again, "Hello? Still there, man? Anyone? Shit..."

In an attempt to ignore the optic abnormality going on in the elevator mirror, he stared at the floor, his head pounding with tension under the indifferent fluorescent light above. The breaths which jolted out of his lungs would not settle, and on a sudden Lewiston thought himself to feel incredibly cold. Temptation overcame him and he looked again at his reflection. This time it was the third reflection that was wrong; *the face wasn't his* - no - this face was one of malice, a look that could precede violence, like a tiger eyeing off its prey moments before the pounce. Lewiston shook his head and began to panic, his heart quickening to a hummingbird speed.

"No, no oh Jesus what the fuck," he looked again.

The reflection nearest to him was not Lewiston at all, rather a malicious shadow of something sinister. The visage of an emaciated, pale man glared ominously at him from behind the glass, its eyes dripping with toxic animosity. The growl of the creature was drowned out by the oncoming scream that peeled from Lewiston's mouth. He wailed desperately as he slammed himself against the elevator doors in a vain attempt to break them open while the apparition continued to watch him with animalistic poise. In his panic Lewiston couldn't comprehend his surroundings and threw himself at the doors until his bones ached. The lights flickered and dimmed for a moment, and when the elevator carriage was illuminated once more, he saw that he was casting no reflection at all. He screamed anew and gave himself away to terror; the lights went out again - longer this time - and when they returned Lewiston was cowering in the corner and sobbing. Silence reigned bar his shallow breathing; even the ventilation fan made no sound, and the buzz of the fluorescent light was no more. Lewiston looked again at the infinity mirror, and everything was as it should be. His eyes darted this way and that - counting the reflections, their orientation, their faces, movement - it was all normal. There was no telling how long he remained staring at those reflections before his composure seemingly returned and he almost uttered a nervous laugh. Lewiston turned away from the mirror and was given no time to scream before the creature grasped his face in an iron grip and he saw no more.

"Are You There?"

It was the third time Davyd Triptych had been asked to work over the weekend that sent him over the edge. Action had to be taken lest he found his ass anchored to the seat of his truck any longer than necessary. He'd finally done it – up and told his boss that he had already planned a holiday for the weekend. A half-truth, perhaps, as the idea had floated through his mind many times in the last month, and it was not as though he was short of cash either; he'd been overworked running the red-eye deliveries across the country (up at sparrow's fart as his father would have said), and had no discretionary time to spend his pay anyway. It appeared that the pressure to work harder had finally gotten Triptych to pursue the opposite and take some time off to recharge.

"Oh, and where are you off to?" his boss had asked.

"The mountains. Bleak Break Peak."

"Well that's a mouthful; say that ten times fast. 'Tis a shame, because I need you working. Times are tough."

No they weren't, thought Triptych, *it's not as though it hits your pocket – there's no bloody overtime pay in this gig!*

"Yarp, that Lady Tenebrific cut funds to the old transportation industry but still expects us to run them deliveries and such."

Me. Not us. It was me running the deliveries while you're at home bouncing that pretty young bird on your lap. How'd he land such a stunner anyway?

"Wish I could be of help but I haven't taken me leave this year. Now's about right."

"Middle of winter," Boss said.

"Yes."

"In the mountains,"

"Yes."

"Well enjoy then." He spun his finger in a circle around his ear and whistled a cuckoo call.

Now Davyd Triptych had two choices then – he could go home and lay low all weekend or he could actually follow through with his little lie and take the M1 up the Jindee Slopes to some cabin where he could lavish in solitude. It seemed an easy choice; being alone was always the easy choice. No need to tell his darling wife where he was off to (for he had no darling wife) and no need to get a friend to check his letterbox whilst he was gone (his truck radio was his only real friend).

"Bleak Break Peak," came the voice on the phone, "this weekend?"

"Yes, is there a problem?"

"Why'dya want that one for? Got plenty of nicer cabins closer to the base."

"No, that one will be just fine."

"Weird bunch some folk are," hissed the man, "ya know it's a blizzard right now?"

"The truck'll handle it."

"Got chains?"

"I've driven through snow before, mate."

"Righto. Hadn't exactly planned to have that cabin set up this weekend but I suppose I can head up there and leave the key and turn the generator on."

Poor you. I'm paying you to holiday at your joint, don't break a leg trying to be hospitable.

Triptych was still irked as his truck rumbled up the highway. At least he'd be away from people for a spell; the hard work had been done – he'd confronted his boss and convinced some grizzled old landowner to rent his least impressive holiday cabin.

Hope the radio works up there. Was it Mariners vs Magpies tonight? Can't remember.

The transmission began to crackle with static as he approached the upper peaks – suddenly it seemed unlikely he'd be listening to any football game tonight. Davyd always found it funny how technology failed in such basic functions. Needn't worry about a signal dropping out when reading a book, no sir, or worry about connections and such whilst scribbling with pencil and paper. Still, if he were to experience the company of humanity at all on his sojourn, he'd hoped it would be the faceless radio presenters.

Can't win 'em all. Least I ain't working.

The road narrowed as he drew nearer to the cabin. He could see the fog lamp shining from the porch; a warmly beacon that ushered him to his destination through the increasing snowfall. He'd been here before, albeit in the summer time, and knew he'd probably need to jump out of the cab to open gate to the driveway. It was a bumpy old drive, barely wide enough for the truck to traverse with the snow drifts spilling into the lane. The headlights illuminated the snow with an unsettling amber hue, and as the iron gate came into view it appeared cold and sterile. Triptych leapt from the cab and into the knee-deep drifts, cursing the sudden and impossible cold. Wading through the snow he gave the gate a good shove, kicking away obstructions and slowly turning it on its hinge. It felt unnecessary, the gate; it was not as if any cattle needed restraining, even in the summer the cows would much prefer the flat, fertile fields lower down the slopes.

Grin and bear. Almost there.

Davyd muttered crossly to himself before chuckling at his unintended rhyme and climbing back into the cab. The lodge came drearily into view betwixt the pines and once Davyd turned the truck engine off he shuddered at the incredible silence that greeted him. As it was the cabin appeared loveless in its isolation; burdened with snow and black windows reflecting the truck headlights with dull disinterest. Sheltered beneath the veranda and doormat, the key was frozen stuck to the floorboards, and Davys swore under his breath as he kicked the thing unstuck and inserted it into the ice-cold lock. The door opened inward with a shuddering groan and the interior met its new inhabitant with the same frigid air as the outdoors. The lights flickered on as though awoken from a deep slumber and Davyd wasted no time in lighting a fire in the hearth. It was a single room, this cabin, so he knew it wouldn't take too long to heat. With those tasks done, exhaustion took him and he collapsed wearily onto the lounge beneath a mass of blankets, the glow of the embers comforting him into a dream-filled sleep.

Davyd Triptych didn't dream often, but when he did, he would find himself just as tired in the morning as when he laid his head down the night before. It was always the same dream; the setting and the people might change, but the scenario remained unchanged – he was running late to work. Maybe he'd slept in, maybe some other obstacle lay in his path, but the story went that he must get to work because the day was wasting away. Sometimes, most grimly, someone he loved had died in this dream, and amongst dream-fed sorrow Davyd choked back tears and reminded himself that he was due at work an hour ago. Then his mouth would drip with blood and he'd spit loose teeth into his palm (would he be able to visit the dentist before work?). He found it bizarre to continually experience the same bad dream, and in this case, he would awake to find it was morning; the overcast light drifting into the cabin windows helped him confirm where he was.

The fire was rekindled and Davyd went about making himself coffee, all the while the silence of the mountains gave subtle hints of its presence – the window panes rattled, the gale moaned, and the cabin creaked under the burden of roof-laden snow. It had been a rough night, a rougher night sleep, but maybe now Davyd Triptych could finally take a deep breath and enjoy his getaway. He stared blankly at the noticeboard that hung in the corner kitchen. It was cork, with flyers and papers pinned to its surface advertising all manner of things. Some flyers were yellowed with age, and Davyd imagined that they had not been updated in some time.

"Thank you for staying at Bleak Break Point, Jindee's hidden gem!"

"Mamma Mazzy's Cardigans and Upholstery – this stitch in time is worth your dime!"

"Passcode for the room safe is 1412" (Now why would they put that in such an obvious place?)

Davyd liked to imagine the time when these posters were relevant, whether Jones & Kindle still had 'the best ski gear this side of the Continent' (or whether Jones & Kindle was still an operating business – given the moth-eaten corners of *that* particular poster, Davyd had to doubt it). The smell of coffee filled him with warmth, and the faded colour posters drew him into a peaceful reverie that was broken by a timid knock on the cabin door. Davyd froze, and the silence that followed led him to wonder if he had in fact heard anything at all. But again there came the same one-two-knock.

A knock tern maybe? No, they don't fly here… But who is knocking on this of all doors?

He stood paralysed, unsure of what to do, a childish fear irrationally washing over him. There was no reason for any other human being to be at this cabin, unless, unless –

Unless it's the proprietor coming to welcome me to his holiday inn?

That was the only thing he could imagine the owner of this knock to be. Davyd moved to the door and reached for the knob.

'Darkness there and nothing more'… Where have I heard that from?

A voice from outside the door sounded, "Are you there?"

Davyd froze once more. The voice, timorous and somewhat higher-pitched, was most certainly *not* the voice of the landowner he had spoken to on the phone the day before. He swallowed hard and stood completely still, as though maybe the mysterious voice would go away if Davyd remained undetected. The gale whistled at the edges of the door and filled the following seconds with ominousness, before the voice came once more, "Hello?" and, "Are you there?"

The truck. Parked outside the cabin. He knows there's someone here. "Are you there?" – how was he to answer such a question? Who was 'you' in this scenario? And who wanted to know?

His behaviour was completely ridiculous. Clearly there was some lost traveller outside his door hoping to find refuge in the cabin. The voice outside uttered a shiver and Davyd heard the faint sound of scratching about the doorframe. On the floor beneath the door Davyd could see the shadow of his visitor moving to the left and to the right, before once more he heard, "Are you there?"

Nothing would come of nothing *(and who had said that?)* and Davyd Triptych realised that he needed to seize control of this situation. Better to attend to this poor lost soul and send him on his way so he could enjoy what remained of his already disrupted holiday. Nonetheless, he snatched up the fire poker in his grasp and held it behind himself as he opened the door. The strange guest had sat himself down on the porch and looked up at Davyd with the excitement that reminded him of a dog that had not seen its master all day. He was a peculiar looking man, pale and thin, with a long face beneath a scalp that was completely bald.

"Oh! There you are!"

"Can I help you?"

"I thought you weren't there," replied the strange man, "thank goodness you are!"

Davyd stared perplexedly at his visitor, "Sorry chap, am I supposed to know who you are?"

"No."

The little bald man continued to flash his empty smile. Davyd frowned down at him, he hated the dominance his stature was giving him, hated the brutish attention it seemed to imply. He offered his hand to the man, allowing him to see the fire poker in the other, just in case he tried anything funny. At full height the visitor was still a foot shorter than Davyd, and he wore little more than a billowing black skivvy and some faded black jeans.

"Jesus man, aren't you cold?" he asked.

"Yes."

Still the man presented his awful smile.

He's clearly a social invalid. Why'd he have to show up here?

"Well come in then, I'll call the proprietor, see if he can't catch you a lift down to the base."

"Oh top! Yes, a lift, that'll do me fine, yes."

The man shuffled into the cabin bringing the cold draft with him, a draft that sent a shudder down Davyd's spine. The door was closed, but still he felt no warmth, something about this weird man rattled his composure. His feet were black, and what Davyd had originally assumed to be shoes were in fact the visitor's frost-bitten bare feet.

"Christ bud! Get those feet by the fire! You'll die of cold at this rate!"

"Okay."

"I'll, uh, call the front office. What's the time, 11? Should be there."

"Okay."

The strange man sat down on the lounge, leaning forward towards the hearth, hands placed awkwardly on his bulbous knee caps. Davyd Triptych had moved to the kitchen.

"You a hiker?" he asked.

The visitor shook his head, "No."

"Staying in one of the lodges around here then?"

"No."

Davyd hissed through his teeth, "Right. So what *are* you doing here then?"

"Warming my feet as you said."

He had not noticed hitherto, but Davyd's heart was thumping hard in his chest, and he realised that this bizarre creature was actually frightening him a little bit.

Don't be stupid, look at him. If he tried anything violent I could easily overpower him.

The fire poker was still in his sweating hand, and Davyd reaffirmed his grip on the handle, unbeknownst to the weird visitor who was humming softly to himself. Davyd picked up the receiver and groaned inwardly at the dull tone that told him the phone was broke. Despite the time, the sky was unusually dark with cloud cover, and Davyd just knew it would soon snow harshly once more. Only in this new fallen darkness did he notice the lamps had gone out, and the only light was the cabin came from the healthy fire crackling indifferently in the hearth.

"Phone's dead, lights are busted. Great."

"It looked important."

"Sorry what?"

The strange man turned to him, "it looked important so I took it."

"Took what?"

"This," the man held up a small object that Davyd recognised as a fuse.

He's bloody mad. I'll bet that's the cabin's fuse right there. He's gone done that on purpose, I know it. I'm stuck here with a bloody mad man. Just relax, we'll sort this out. Small talk, small talk. Get him talking.

"Umm, coffee perhaps?"

"No." the weird man returned to staring at the fire.

My gun. It's in my bag. The cigar box. Bugger me, it's on his side of the room!

"Well I definitely need my coffee," said Davyd, "and I always need a smoke. Say pal, could you hand me that little wooden box there?"

Without hesitation, the strange man picked up the cigar box and handed it to Davyd. A gush of relief coursed through his veins as he concealed the revolver in his pocket; he felt much safer then. He turned to the kitchen bench and began to absent-mindedly make a fresh pot of coffee, glancing over his shoulder every now and then to make sure his little *friend* stayed put.

God I'm a rotten bad actor. He knows I don't trust him, surely.

Davyd grasped his new coffee cup in both hands, the warmth of it grounding him in the reality of his situation. He leant on the kitchen bench, eyeing his visitor, wondering if he was a lunatic escaped from an asylum or just some poor man delusional with hypothermia. Logic told Davyd to stop being so bloody paranoid and suspect the latter. Best to keep up the chatter, get a better read on the guy. Needless to say, his holiday was effectively ruined – people ruined everything!

Outside the snow began to fall heavily.

"Once this passes I'll drive you down the mountain, say?" said Davyd, "Got someone you can call once we get there?"

The strange man turned in his seat to face him, "I think so."

Does he understand me? Maybe this ain't his first language? Geez that would make him a rarity. Not met many who don't know the major language. Ask something simple.

"What's your name?"

The strange man seemed to consider for a moment, "I am... Alone Again."

"No, your name, son. What is your name?"

"You can call me... Jones. Cardigan Jones."

Davyd Triptych's heart began to beat furiously once more.

That confirms it. The man has to be a criminal. Cardigan Jones? No-one is named that! His eyes. Horrible empty eyes. That smile can't hide it. What's he looking at me like that for? He's not looking at me. He's looking at the corkboard behind me.

He turned to read some of the flyers again. They fluttered as innocently as they had before, although now there was a distinct illness in those moth-eaten edges – a decay that dulled colours and made certain words stand out more than others, words that spoke of Mamma Mazzy's *Cardigans*…. Of *Jones* & Kindle….

Of course. A pseudonym. This had to be the way I'd go out – murdered in a bloody cabin in the woods. I'll be a damn folk tale. I had to be a red-headed man, too – those blokes always got killed first in horror movies.

Davyd grabbed the car keys off the kitchen bench and pondered his next move. Just get away, that's all he had to do. Pretend to drive down to the base to get help, and then piss bolt away from these mountains forever.

"Might turn that truck engine over; will freeze if I don't. I'll drive on down to the reception cabin, you can wait here."

He turned from the bench and found Cardigan Jones no longer sitting by the fireplace but standing a few feet away with all the silence and rigidity of a statue. The smile was upon his face no longer, replaced with an empty glare that ramped up Davyd's heart rate further.

"I like your beard."

Composure was rapidly dissipating from Davyd as an instinct foreign and almost animalistic kicked in. Flashes of memories long past flew by his third eye; he recalled a time when he was a boy when he'd almost drowned in the local dam before his friend had pulled him above the water. It was odd to him to recall that now, a frightful memory he'd long repressed, but this new fear coursing in his veins had unearthed it. He saw the dark waters of that dam in the eyes of the strange man, whose eyes positively dripped with increasing malice.

"You remind me of him. Daddy Long-Legs." Jones said.

"Look man," Davyd stumbled, "no idea what you're saying to me. I'm going to leave you for just a minute, yeah? No point us both going out in the cold. Let me grab someone who can help you. I'll be back in half hour tops."

He stared back at the man, this Cardigan Jones, and warily awaited his reaction. If he could get to the door, it'd be all over. He stuck his hands into his coat pockets – as casually as he could – and clutched the reassuring handle of the revolver. Cardigan Jones just stared and stared, the corner of his lip quivering as he wriggled his fingers by his sides.

"Oh, you could help me," he answered at last, "I only need one thing."

One thing. Should I bite? Is he trying to trap me?

"My headache. I need you to take it away."

"You – your headache? Got some tablets you could take in the first aid box…."

"No," Jones interrupted, "No not like that. My head hurts. My headache; I need *you* to take it."

"I don't understand you, man."

"I said take it! Argh my head!"

Cardigan Jones launched himself at Davyd Triptych. Before he could react, Davyd felt his wrist grasped in an inhumanely strong grip. He gasped and struggled to snatch the gun from his coat but his attacker had already disarmed him with his impossible strength. Jones wrapped his other hand about Davyd's neck as he was subdued to the floor, Davyd left wondering how this gaunt and seemingly malnourished man could be so strong.

"Take my pain," roared the visitor, "I can't stand it anymore."

Those empty and horrible eyes bulged further, the veins in Cardigan's neck throbbing with violence. Davyd gaped for air but the man would not ease up his grip; he had to act soon before he passed out. With his one free arm he groped blindly about himself, grabbing the fire poker he'd had previously in his grasp and giving it an almighty swing. The impact rung through the cabin with a dull clanging as Davyd was afforded a brief second to free himself from the stunned attacker. He shoved Cardigan Jones to the ground and raced for the door, fumbling for the car keys before he felt that vice grip once more – this time around his ankle. He kicked at his attacker's head but nothing seemed to hurt the freak. Then, remembering an old trick his father had taught him, he held the keys in his closed fist with the point poking betwixt two fingers and threw a punch that crushed Cardigan's eye. The attacker reeled and screamed, the keys still lodged in the socket, as Davyd dashed out the door and into the knee-deep snow. No truck, he'd have to get away on foot. He ran blindly through the trees, howling curses at the elements – the snow that impeded his progress, the terrain that sloped and dropped and provided limited footing and the silence of the woods that amplified the sounds of his struggles. He tripped and fell down an icy slope, the traction beneath him all gone, and slid across a frozen creek bed before coming to a stop. His blood smeared the ice as he lay there; a gash across his head and a dislocated elbow seemed to be his only injuries. Davyd looked back up the hill from where he'd come. The cabin was completely out of sight, his adrenaline-charged escape had taken him a mile or so away from his attacker. Cardigan Jones was nowhere to be seen, yet Davyd could hear the horrid moaning of the creep some distance up the hill, a moaning that broke into the most chilling and grief-choked sobbing he had ever heard in his life.

Tower of Fog

The sun rose, and through the veil of mist, threw its rays with furious abandon at the cloud that perennially coated the mountains. These mountains wound along the bleak coast, corroded fangs weathered by the lashings of sea foam, as stone grey as the sky that stood over them like a loveless parent. They crawled from the earth with the ocean salivating at their heels and reached, reached for the nurturing warmth of sunlight. But the fog remained, the sun set again, and all was lost in eternal monochrome. The northern tower jutted crudely from the peaks, needle-thin, so that the wind that rushed about its zenith whistled like a tuning fork.

In the highest room of the tower, where joviality was given up to the valleys of echoes, Greywaite sat atop a stool. He was of crumbled carriage, as though the oceanic air had weathered his posture inasmuch as the disintegrating horizons surrounding the tower. His white hair receded like waves on a domed beach, slithering backwards from his scalp in lengthy serpents that tumbled floor-bound. Beneath the layers of beard and hair, his cloak bloated about his shapeless form. The navy blue of this cloak, so muted that one must look twice to confirm the presence of any colour at all, pertained to Greywaite's ghostly ensemble, yet added little worth to the stormy gloom of the room. He had waited all night, and now the morning crept upon the tower. The transition towards light was one sluggish and subtle; the overcast sky seemingly dragging the daylight back towards night. It was not as though Greywaite noticed the morning anyway; he merely stared from the window of that airy room out across the peaks to the southern tower that stood in the distance. His eyes were searching, yet old age appeared to have limited his ability to do so. When the yearning for his vision to focus upon the other tower became too frustrating, he turned his gaze to the floor and sighed heavily. The fraying wires of his mind had shot currents betwixt each other in an attempt to comprehend his depression, depression that turned to irritation as a knock sounded at his door.

"Enter."

The door groaned ajar and a figure stepped in, though this figure was somewhat ignored by Greywaite, who continued to stare from the window.

For several seconds, there was only the sound of laborious breathing in the room.

"It is you, Flagcloak?"

"The same you would see."

Greywaite turned his head slightly, so that little more than his profile could be discerned from Flagcloak's position. The visitor was of similar stature to the man by the window; perhaps age had been a touch kinder on his rugged features, his shock of hair maintained the golden glow of youth, and coupled with a beard shorter than that of Greywaite, he carried a lion-like appearance. It was from his cracked mouth that the exhalations of a man exhausted exhume, for he had climbed the corroded spiral of stairs to its very summit in order to pay visit to Greywaite. Had Flagcloak not climbed the steps once a day, who else would there be to see him? In spite of the lonesome outpost in which Greywaite perched himself like some crestfallen eagle, Flagcloak, his sole companion, still readily appeared once a day to visit.

The leonine man began to circle the room and admired the dusty ornaments that lined the shelves with a most steady patience. His digits stroked the spines of moth-eaten tomes and caressed the plumage of a stuffed falcon perched lifelessly on the shelf. Flagcloak coughed, for the dust unsettled from some ashen snow globe had permeated his nostrils and surrounded him in a ghostly shroud.

Greywaite, as though only just remembering that he had company, spoke. "I saw him again last night."

Flagcloak turned and followed the aquiline nose of the elderly vulture to where it pointed beyond the open window. "And how did the night fare?"

"My night was..."

Here Greywaite grew frustrated at the very idea of speech, and wished only to tear at his own voice box until silence conquered. He grunted and felt his shoulders droop. His lips parted slightly and from his throat he made to speak again; he fought against his abhorrence and attempted to croak new notes in his birdsong once more.

"As it is every night," he began. "That charlatan. That supercilious apparition – taunting me with its deafness. Every night, Flagcloak. I see that ghost in the southern tower, from the window level with my own. It is but the only light lower than the stars, yet it glows from the highest room of that wicked tower."

"The face, my friend?" replied Flagcloak.

Greywaite snorted, face twisting with disgust. "Ah that face! Staring deadpan from those horrible black eyes. Ignoring any signal of mine to engage with it. Is he so much conceited that he cannot acknowledge me? So long have I sat friendless in this tower, and he mocks me with his staring."

The pair, though not of any conscious accord, switched positions as Flagcloak paced to the window. Greywaite slumped from his stool and leaned heavily upon his writing desk, as though to pour fury from his very beard.

"Had you not thought of going there and uncovering the wight yourself?" Flagcloak asked.

"When he may do the same?" Greywaite retorted, and then calmed. "The perspective, Flagcloak. You do not understand. I have never been to the southern tower. To stand in place of that ghost, to see my dear northern tower from another vantage point... No, I could not."

Greywaite drew beside Flagcloak and gazed at the southern tower, where the window of the accused apparition gaped – a blackened maw.

"A horrifying thought," he muttered.

Flagcloak eyed the old man perplexedly. "Perhaps tomorrow a change will come," he said.

The cease of speech accentuated the sounds of silence; waves hushed in distant din, and about the pinnacle of southern tower the shrill bell-cry of the seagulls rang sempre forte. Those gulls, spinning as though on the strings of a mobile, would soon drift from the tower and plunge sea-bound with the encroaching night. This Greywaite knew, and as such did not acknowledge them. Readily he returned to the writing desk and allowed his face to droop into his arms – his features contorted with self-inflicted torture. Flagcloak let his vision glass over as the hypnotic gulls sung and glided about the other tower. The light entering through the window illuminated his features – that white and static light held him as a flame embraces a moth.

"The birds..." came Greywaite's muffled voice.

Flagcloak drifted slowly from his reverie. "Hmm?"

"The birds return with the daylight."

With a sigh that shook the dust from his shoulders, Greywaite rapped an impatient fist against his desk, then absently traced the corroded brickwork patterns of the wall before him. An involuntary twitch shivered down his back, and he turned to observe Flagcloak's vacant eyes pouring into him.

"Why do you stare so?"

"Hmm?"

"I... would like to be alone," said Greywaite.

"Would you?" replied Flagcloak.

The two men stared at one another in a seemingly eternal stand-off before Flagcloak broke his gaze, and with little more than a sleight of his hand, pocketed a small item in his cloak – a single match – before heading for the door.

"Until the morrow."

Greywaite did not respond, and returned to the windowsill where the southern tower taunted him with its presence.

Out on the threshold, Flagcloak shivered. The cold hanging dismally over the mountains had not withheld itself from Greywaite's airy room, yet the gusts blowing unabated against the outside walls cut deep into Flagcloak's bones with a new menace. The peaks jutted in serrated hostility, stretching far in three directions. To the west, the sea moaned with the gale, and as Flagcloak began his descent of the spiral stairs, he felt naught but discomfort. The steps coiled about the exterior of the northern tower like an ivy vine, and Flagcloak could not balance himself on any sort of handrail. To his left, the oyster-sharp wall crumbled with erosion. To the right — a sickening precipice. As such his pace was sluggish, and though no sunlight told of the remaining hours of day, he knew he must move somewhat faster if he had any hope of beating the night.

Onward he trudged, a vapid spectre in the approaching dusk. From his rattling lungs came a wheeze of exertion, steadily breaking with the sound of shore-struck waves. Flagcloak moved as swiftly as his archaic legs would allow, his bare and calloused feet gripping tenaciously against the rocky path that crested the sea cliffs.

He arrived at an overhang of rock that hid the entrance of a dank cave. Mechanically he took an old lantern hanging from a rusted hook just within his reach. Assailed on all sides by the roar of the ocean echoing off the cave walls, he fumbled with the match procured from his pocket, and despite the moist and loveless air, was able to ignite his lantern. He cast an awful shadow, one hunched and distorted against the cave walls, warping madly as the flame flickered in the oceanic chaos. The sickly orange glow sank further into the cave, until those remaining birds huddled for warmth near the cave mouth were left in the darkness.

Flagcloak began an ascent as treacherous as that descent from the north tower, fumbling through the gloom up each slimy step; all the while the waters below growled hungrily for him to plummet into the maw. But this was a journey that Flagcloak knew too well. In time he noticed strange shapes forming in his peripherals; a curious light seemed to lurk menacingly outside the range of the dingy lantern, and Flagcloak realised he was close. That curious light was in fact the moon, which signalled his way out of the upper entrance of the cave and up a spiralled stairwell, from which moonlight poured through adorning windows. Round he went, up the steps – seeing now the waxing lunar orb cutting the gluttonous shadows of each protruding stone, and now the inky pitch which consumed the next turn as he climbed the spiral.

Finally, battered and exhausted, Flagcloak reached the small room he called home. He hung the lantern on the wall by the window, so that the flames contoured every crevasse of his cracked skin, and shadows blackened the globules of his eyes. Flagcloak took a seat upon a stool by the window, from where he could see the distant northern tower, and the hideous figure of Greywaite staring back at him with oblivious hatred.

The Shaman

"Will."

Silence.

"Lee."

Silence.

"Wag-Tail."

Silence.

"Willie Wagtail."

"Yes?"

"Why didn't you answer me the first time?"

"You only said my name once."

"No I didn't. I said it twice. Once was slow."

"The slow was incorrect."

"Does it matter?"

"What's the matter?"

"You're the matter."

"I am matter."

"So are you."

"That's what I said."

"Tis still rude to be silent."

Silence.

"Now you're ignoring me. I called your name."

"You didn't say a thing."

"My point exactly."

"You may have yerself a name, but I gots a title."

"The Shaman? He he. Give us yer dog-end."

"No."

"Give us a toke?"

"That's the same thing."

"Pfft."

"Ye got a name and I don't, and now ye want my smoke? It's my only one."

"You're holding another."

"No I'm not."

"Behind yer ear."

"Ears can't hold."

"Stands to reason."

Silence.

"It's raining."

"No it isn't."

"It is somewhere."

"So it still is?"

"How would I know?"

Silence.

"It's foggy."

"Very foggy."

"Thick as soup."

"Unless it's broth."

"Also true."

The silence was at last broken by the loud cackle of kookaburras in the distant woodlands. The Shaman had always seen those particular birds as harbingers of rainfall, but given how often it rained in Norfolk this was hardly prophetic. His companion, Willie Wagtail, rose from the boulder which served as his seat and brushed dirt from his coat. Why he bothered to do so when his clothes were beyond filthy made the Shaman chuckle inwardly. Wagtail faced the Shaman, who was still seated, and poked a begrimed finger at his chest.

"Wazzat?"

Shaman looked down and Wagtail flicked him on the nose and took the cigarette from behind his ear.

"Bastard!"

It was the oldest trick in the book, and he'd fallen for it. Willie Wagtail triumphantly lit the cigarette, puffed proudly and handed it back to the Shaman.

"Was saving that."

"Ne'er mind, dear."

"How am I supposed to get more smokes now?"

"Tomorrow we die, love. Smoke away."

"Someone's coming."

Along the country road that smelt of mud and rainwater, the droplets flickered on the surface of puddles as a few lazy frogs poked their eyes above the ooze and groaned, and a new pair of figures appeared on the scene to bring change to the stagnant countryside. Wagtail pulled a switchblade from his coat and shuddered at the delightful click of the blade snapping into place. The Shaman impatiently waved him away.

"Kids, Will. No need for that."

The two kids had seen the vagabonds loitering under their dead tree, and seemed to slow their pace as they approached. Time seemed to be weighed down by the mud; the boggy ground slowed their progress furthermore, its sticky grasp threatening to suck their boots into the earth. It was a girl and a boy, and to Shaman and Wagtail, neither of them looked as though they had anything worth stealing on them. As they drew nearer, the kids seemed to gather confidence, and the boy took a noble stride ahead of the girl and faced them with a feebly-construed fearlessness.

"We're looking for the Shaman's house," he said.

The two vagabonds glanced at one another.

"Well," said the Shaman, "Fi were you, I'd be reading that sign yonder," he thumbed at a small wooden post driven into the ground just beyond the dead tree.

The girl read the sign, "Hmm, *'Shaman's house 2 kms. No solisitters.'* Reckon this guy never finished school."

Willie Wagtail snorted with laughter before doubling over as the Shaman shoved an elbow into his ribs. The boy looked excitedly about himself and shook the rainwater from his dirty little head.

"So we're nearly there?"

The Shaman shrugged, "So the sign says,"

"Thank you!"

The kids continued on until they disappeared into the distant woodlands.

"Where do they get that?" asked Wagtail.

"Eh?"

"The vigour. The energy. Where do they get it?"

"We all had it once, deary. Tis siphoned out. One day yer correcting the spelling of yer elders, and the next..."

They returned to their silent post beneath the tree, the thin smoke trail of the Shaman's cigarette climbing skyward as though it were an extension of his person, merging into the moist air surrounding. Wagtail kicked his foot rhythmically and sucked on his teeth to pass the time. Time, however was seemingly refusing to move, as though it had stopped on its path to observe the two strange men who threatened to kill it with their passivity. Yes, time was being killed slowly by the gentlemen, and time could do little but gaze deer-stunned into the eyes of its predator.

"Suppose those kids..."

"They'll be back, Will; if that is in fact, the case."

"Yeah."

Silence.

"Might rob ya." said Wagtail.

"How's that?"

"Told 'em where you live."

"How's that?"

"Well, you're here. Yer house there. Unattended."

"Don't matter."

"How's that?"

"Because I'm here."

"How's that?"

"And me house is there."

"How's that?"

"Well if I'm here and the kids are there, they can hardly rob *me*, who is *here*."

"Rob yer house, you beautiful idiot."

"Oh.... Yer should've said."

"I did!"

"No matter. The kids return."

Along the trail, in a mirrored occurrence of their previous passing, the boy and the girl trudged back towards the Shaman and Willie Wagtail. The youthful vigour they'd shown had now slumped into a perfunctory amble, for the hour that had passed by since the kids first passed had gone unnoticed by the two gentlemen sitting under the tree.

"Find the house?" asked Wagtail.

"He wasn't home," replied the boy.

"Could've told you that," said the Shaman.

"You knew?" asked the girl.

"He would."

"How's that?"

"He *is* the Shaman."

The boy and the girl let out a gasp mingled with a multitude of tones; frustration, for why hadn't the man mentioned that he was the Shaman; humiliation, for their journey had become longer than it needed to be; relief, for they had at last found who they were looking for.

"You're the Shaman?" asked the boy.

"In the flesh."

"Why didn't you tell us?" asked the girl.

"Ye never asked."

"We asked you where the Shaman's house was."

"And I answered truthfully."

"Yes. But. You. Oh!" here the boy's apparent frustration welled into a sob, and the young girl clasped her friend's shoulders as he cried.

"Nice one, Sham," said Wagtail, "made a kiddly-wink cry."

"Surely I didn't," the Shaman replied, "he cries at the futility of his quest. The delay of his Eden. Led down the muddy river of Styx when the tree of knowledge stands right here." Here he gestured to the dead tree upon which they leant.

"Enough riddles!" snapped the girl, "You are the Shaman – yes or no?"

"I am known as the Shaman, yes."

"You can answer the questions we have then."

"I can answer most anything – but Lor' bless you, I ain't always right."

The boy dried his eyes and nose on his sleeve and procured a crumpled photograph from his pocket, "My name is Rheneas. My brother Balfour has gone missing."

"Been lost for years meself, boy," said the Shaman, "mayhaps I'm the brother you seek?"

"What? No! Here!"

He thrust the photograph at the Shaman, but would not let him take it from his grasp. The picture was, at present, all that linked him to Balfour, and Rheneas had no intention of relinquishing it.

"Ain't seen him lad. Not many come by here."

"We've come," said the girl (who by now, it should be known, was Pidgee), "because we heard you might know about the Norfolk Wights."

The vagabonds shuddered and crossed themselves. Wagtail began to pace nervously about, and the Shaman looked this way and that, as if avoiding eye contact with his interrogator would refute the question.

"Thas a devil's expression, missy."

Pidgee pressed on; the reaction of these two old clowns gave her immediate hope that they knew something that she did not, "We saw them just outside our home town. The ghosts. The two of us and Rhen's brother. Balfour, he tried to take a photograph of them and…"

"And them ghosties didn't like it," said the Shaman.

"Yes!" quipped Rhen, "and next we knew, my brother was gone, and so were the Wights."

Here Rheneas broke into sobs once more, "Oh mister please say you know what happened. Tell me my bro is ok, that you know something – *anything*."

The Shaman was touched; rarely did anybody show him respect, let alone refer to him as 'mister'. Wagtail however, continued to shuffle about nervously; the presence of this weeping child made him somewhat uncomfortable.

"He sees," said Willie Wagtail.

"He does," replied the Shaman.

"Behemoth hates Leviathan."

"Who in turn hates the other."

"Ocean beat against the land."

"And land returns another," here he turned to Rheneas, "Son I'll tell ya. I know about them ghosties. Know 'em good. I was once a resident of yer humble township; made my abode by the fish docks on the lower side."

"Really?" said Pidgee, "I've never seen you before."

The Shaman nudged Wagtail, "Ye hear this one, Will? *She's* never seen me before. Then I must not exist – yep it's gospel."

Wagtail chuckled.

"I'll get to it, missy," continued the Shaman, "but Lor' bless ya I lived in Norfolk long before ye were a twinkle in yer old man's eye. Lived me youth, lived me adolescence, lived me *sane* adulthood in that little town – pretty thing it was. God, I miss it. Brother and I used to clean the catch on an evening – too prone to seasickness was my brother, and I wasn't one to leave him behind. Honest work it was, though I reckon I'm still scrubbing the fish stink off me today. Yep, a pimple on the sweet buttock of an angel, I was. But I knew I'd never truly enjoy any whimsy for my toil. Ye know the kind – clean bed, warm walls, full belly. I'll bet you kids wouldn't know the half of what sufferin' can be. But that's beside the point. Point is my brother says one day, he says 'bro, there's ghosts on yonder hill outside town.' And I see by the glint in yer glance, boy, that my tale may be a twistin' its similarities into yours. Now I hadn't lived under no rock (not *literally*, at least) to have no knowledge of the Norfolk Wights. Can't pass up a single Halloween without someone telling the tale once more. But me? I'd had just about enough of tall stories. How was it that others could accrue wealth while I scrambled for my scraps? How, when even the most noble of Norfolkians was afraid o' ghosts? Well I says to my dear bro, 'bro, I'm off to prove the Wights ain't nothing but a hoax.'"

Silence.

"And?" Rhen asked.

"And that was the last time I saw him."

"He's one for drama, ain't he," said Wagtail, "Saw him again, buggerhead."

The Shaman sighed, "Was going for a bit of poetic licence, fool. Lemme finish. So, this little proclamation of mine came at an opportune time, for you see I wasn't the best tenant and the old landlord decided he'd had a gutful of me. And by that, I mean the cops approached me in the threshold of my favourite alley and told me to move along. So, I packs up me stuff and pitch the tent up on them hills outside of town. Ye know the ones. The ones where them ghosties are spooking. I stayed there better part of a week, I did – not one apparition blesses me with his or her presence. Course it was pissing rain that whole time, but I didn't care; was out to prove a point after all. But one day rolls around and the sweet sun kisses me sodden head. 'Clear skies it be! Tonight's the night!' I says. Had no idea I'd have such anticipation, but I did – was right nervous all day. Evening rolls round and absolutely nothin' happens. I'm sitting propped up against a tree with my campfire slowly dwindling, and me a 'nodding off to sleep. Must've been around midnight I wake with a start – fire's dead and all around there's this minty green glow; like fog it was, only brighter, if you can understand. And I'm not proud to say, but I'm afraid at this point. For there's the ghosties in the flesh – or in the plasm, whatever – descending upon me! I sees the shapes of these nasty things looming closer and closer, the height of two men and eyes that could freeze ye very heart in place."

There was a moment of silence.

"What happened next?" asked Rhen, wide-eyed.

The Shaman shuffled on his perch; even Willie Wagtail, who'd heard this story many times before, stood with piqued interest.

"Well, hard to say," continued the Shaman, "I remember a lot of darkness. I remember time sort of disappearing – couldn't have told you if it was Sunday or February. And when I'd finally regained the cognitive function of 'membering what was what, I was wandering through the bushlands who-knows-where, and finally reach this dingy little settlement. Just a main street, couple of buildings. Clearly just a pit stop for those on longer sojourns, ye know?

"I enter the smithy shack, must be fairly early of a morn, man there is banging away at his forge – only one of several scattered folk in that there town. I must've been a sight, for most of 'em ignored me. Anyway, smithy man asks of me purpose and I says 'where are we?' Well, he goes 'Mid-North, ten miles west o' the junction to Jindee,'

"Blimey! I says, I'm on the other side of the bloody Continent! And sir, I says, what year is it? Right now he's looking at me like I've two heads and says 'Why it's the year of our Lord such-and-such' to which I realise I been wandering in the fog for six years! No fooling!"

"Sounds pretty unbelievable to me...." said Pidgee.

Wagtail shrugged and the Shaman sighed, "Well, you're just tough to please ain't ya, missy?"

"Did you go back home then?" asked Rhen.

"That was the first thought, of course. I'd never been too far from Norfolk until then, so I didn't know which was up or down. But I took to wandering as easily as slumming it in an alley. I knows how to live it rough, as I hope you see. Rest of the story is a tad less spectacular; shall we say? I returned to Norfolk, where everyone had assumed me dead for years, even me bro. Sadly enough I learn me bro finally overcame his fear of the ocean and had set off on a big old boat long before my return. And you know the people in

Norfolk – Lor bless ya, ye are people from Norfolk – well thems being the superstitious lot took me for a spectre, and those less fearful thought I was some raving derelict and chased me outta town. You know how they feels about ghosties."

"So then what happened?"

The Shaman laughed, "found myself this lovely rock" (he patted the boulder) "next to this lovely tree" (he gestured to the dead tree) "and have sat here ever since."

"How long?" asked Rhen.

"Cor, I don't know, friend," he replied, "I live in a shack in the forest. You think I know what the time is?"

Willie Wagtail chimed in, "Us hobos can count the sunrises and sunsets – but after a while ye lose count. Then you realise 'tis pointless to count 'em anyhow."

A short silence overcame them. The breeze rattled the branches of the dead tree, and a frog crawled from a nearby puddle, before Pidgee broke the quiet, "But wait!"

"She ruins me poetic effect again, she does," sighed the Shaman.

"Not one for artistry, love," replied Wagtail.

"Shoosh!" snapped Pidgee, "You didn't tell us what happened to the Wights! Or anything about Rhen's brother!"

"I told ye everything I know, and I'd wager everything you need to know."

"How'd you figure?" asked Pidgee.

"Well matey, I saw the Wights and I live today," he turned to Rheneas, "so I'd bet me ample fortune that your brother is alive, and well and truly fine – just somewhere else!"

Brooding Over Brews

Go and collect yourself.

It was surely an innocuous command, yet for Orion – who was prone to reading too far into things – those words uttered by his wife Sabina seemed cloaked in a subtle venom. Orion had not been coping; that much was obvious even to strangers in the coffee house, let alone his wife and best friend – the mother of his five-day old son. The new father had not been outdoors in over a week and as such had winced with weary eyes under the overcast sky that hung above the coastal town of Estoram. The rain had fallen in cold daggers on his shoulders but Orion hadn't minded that one bit. It was a welcome change to the claustrophobic confines of his home, confines that were wrapped in the tired cries of a newborn baby like so many spider web threads. The cold weather reminded him that he was alive; he was never one to understand how a person could prefer the insufferable summer months over the milder seasons. And now, with the rain having steadily increased in the half hour he had been brooding in the local coffee house Orion felt somewhat normal for the first time in a long while. But in being a man of gentle temperament he could not help but allow guilt to stain that normalcy he was feeling; his wife was still at home and would be for some time, wrestling with the unforeseeable stresses of becoming a parent.

Should I really be here? Orion had thought, pondering his age-old pastime that sat before him in a china cup. The comforting smells of coffee might revive him for a short while, help him *collect* himself, but his new responsibility would be there when he returned home, wrapped like a little present in blankets. Surely this was a creature comfort that he could no longer *afford*. How could a creature comfort serve its purpose when he knew his generous wife suffered the same qualm at home – rather she was forced to burden it alone while her husband *collected* himself.

We can only afford one insane family member at a time, my love.

There was that word again: *afford*. It stung Orion to hear it; even though they had gone over the numbers and confirmed that yes, they could afford to live off of his wage alone, his naturally fretful mind felt an immense pressure that was mostly self-inflicted. Why did it trouble him so? He'd proven time and again to be a savvy saver – almost to the point of becoming miserly. Life had hurled its challenges at him and he'd gotten through it all so far, why would this be any different?

Because there is a helpless little dependent at stake now.

Because now another would suffer should he fail. Orion was always a man to bear the weight of his failures, take their lessons in stock and bounce back better the next time. Parenthood had been more difficult than he had imagined. *It gets better* – the adage quipped to him by many who had *been there, done that*. But *better* was *later*, what of *now*? He sipped at his espresso and stared at the rain-stained window and the street beyond. An emaciated tree branch scratched at the glass as though begging an entry into the warm cafe. Orion ignored it and was instead entranced by the raindrops that slid down the sleek pane. The weight of each droplet dragged earthbound and he imagined that weight pressing slowly on his own shoulders too. It was the weight of his own burdens – not a load that will crush its bearer all at once, rather a slow poison or gravity that constricted until he would be no longer able to stand it. Orion thought of a moment in his childhood when his father had pointed out a certain vine that grew in abundance around his home. As a boy he had liked the look of the sinuous plant, curling this way and that through the flowers and tree trunks, up power lines and latching to brick walls. But his father had warned him of such parasitic plants and how they weakened the very lynchpins on which they clung. A sadness crept through Orion's heart whenever he saw his father severing the roots of those vines, even though he implored his son that it was better to pick your battles or risk a slow demise. Had Orion allowed his burden to grow too heavy? It was too late to reconsider that now; to even entertain such a thought made his heart burst with love for his little son. Everyone had told him that the birth of a child was incomparable, and he had not understood that statement until it had happened to him personally. Which was all the more reason why his anxiety escalated – he just wanted the world for his kin.

Those thoughts led Orion to throwing back the remainder of his coffee and cursing inwardly; what was he doing here? Parents weren't supposed to indulge in their own pleasures, were they? No, that was an exaggeration. He knew now that he was overthinking things. A happy man would make for a more efficient parent. Yes, it was right for his wife to have sent him away like this; the fresh air had done him good and he felt a renewed vigour towards the new challenges of his life. He would not allow his wife or son to struggle unnecessarily, and this attitude alone was enough for him to ensure he would see through his ambitions. Orion would be the bearer of any burden if it meant that his family knew happiness. Having reached this agreeable conclusion with his inner demons, his mind began to drift into the mesmerising din of the cafe. To some, this coffee house was a little too dank to really enjoy; the air was rank with sour scents of cigarette and old grounds, but to others these smells brought such comforts that might be felt by a child who adores a certain blanket and refuses to wash it. Floored by chequered tiles of black and white turned grey it was a place where one could easily drift into a trance, lulled by the white noise of clinking glasses and the grinding coffee machine. A television screen hung in a corner above the bar, and Orion now fixed his gaze on it, where a large woman was being interviewed. Orion was in a bit of a stupor – these television screens had been a fairly recent invention and he hadn't seen too many of them before; in all honesty it came as a surprise that the coffee house proprietor could afford one.

"Ah, turn that crap off!" came a gruff shout.

"Can it, Rodney. It cost a mint to get it installed," replied the barista Suzan.

"Damn pollies'll be the death of me. 'Fi wanted to hear from this bitch I read the papers! 'Least then I don't gotta hear her voice."

Suzan sighed, "*You'll* be the death of *me*, Rod. I never should have gotten that damn liquor license."

Orion had become enraptured in their exchange and with the cafe being rather low on patrons this particular afternoon, he listened like a fly on the wall.

Rodney smirked at Suzan, seemingly forgetting the television for a moment, "Carn love. Can't I have a beer?"

"You can," said Suzan, "but you've had far more than one, my friend."

"Well blame that pisher Ryan down the road!"

Suzan began cleaning coffee cups, "He kicked you out for being too drunk. You're lucky I don't do the same."

"Fine," huffed Rodney; he was too drunk to continue the argument, "how's about a coffee then?"

"Black, no sugar it is,"

"You're a sweet lass,"

"And you're a right ass, Rodney," chuckled Suzan.

She called over to Orion, "How about you, mate? Another?"

Orion flushed on a sudden, embarrassed that she might have caught him eavesdropping, "Uh, yes maybe just one more."

The man named Rodney sat with shoulders slouched, stirring a sugar into his coffee. The years he had wasted drunk bore a heavy strain on his weather-beaten face, but now that he was an old bastard, good-for-nothing alco he figured that he may as well resign himself to his fate. There were few beyond the walls of the cafe that would bother to listen to him.

"Damn Tenebrific," he was almost in tears, "sending me broke, she is. Hits us tax payers hard."

Suzan snorted, "Now you're rambling again – you ain't worked a day in years."

She moved away from the counted with Orion's coffee and placed it down in front of him. The barista looked older now that she stood closer to him, older than perhaps she should. Too much work and too little sleep – Orion could relate. Readjusting the strings of her apron, Suzan coughed discreetly, not wanting to appear unclean around her customers; that was lesson one in hospitality. Glancing at her wrist watch she moved hastily to the door and closed it, preventing the rain and further customers from entering.

"Almost quitting time, folks," she called to the scant few people remaining in the shop.

Suzan and Rodney continued their political exchange while Orion listened, yet the eavesdropper could tell that neither of them were very knowledgeable in regards to the subject. Orion knew the woman on the television screen – Libra Tenebrific, the leader of Verdigris and incumbent in the upcoming election; he had seen her picture in the papers plenty of times.

"You're not wrong about her, Rod," sighed Suzan, "she'll continue to be bad news if she stays in power."

Pondering his new fatherhood, of which Ms Tenebrific knew nothing of, Orion cringed to think of the unknown future that lay before him. It was true that he was capable of supporting his family on his humble wage, but Tenebrific's policies made her a tough sell to a middle-class man like himself. The rich got richer under her reign, and unfortunately the opposition in Austen Spindle offered little to appeal to Orion. While Spindle promised a better turn of fortune for society's strugglers, those in the middle – neither rich or poor – were being left high and dry, stuck between a rock and a hard place.

Orion tossed back his coffee and made a move towards the door; the rain had stopped and fortune said it would not hold out for long. The walk to his house was short, but mostly on a steep incline, and sure as he had thought, the rain began to fall again shortly after he left the cafe. He pulled his coat over his head and began to run, eyes fixed on the pavement before him out of fear of slipping. As such he took no time to admire his simple but pretty home, its corrugated iron roof, the unkempt rose bushes choking the chipped white paint of the front veranda. For a fleeting moment he thought about checking the mail box but readily decided against it – it would only be bills if anything, and they could get soaked through for all he cared. Orion's frantic dash home would then turn into a mission of stealth, as he slowly nudged the front door open and cursed the dull groan of its hinges. A single light globe shone in his threshold, throwing shadows across photographs of his wife and the bouquets of flowers given to them in celebration of their new baby. The house was silent, with little more to be heard than the droplets hitting the roof above – the baby must be asleep. Striding slowly into the sitting room he drank in the tranquil scene of his wife ensconced in a large arm chair, the fireplace highlighting the lines on her face that told of contented fatigue. And in her arms was not a sleeping child as Orion had thought, rather his son was in fact wide awake and gazing about the room with that disjointed fixation that brightened the eyes of all newborns. *Awake but not crying! The very thought!* Orion sighed heavily and prayed that his intrusion would not break the scene.

"You're home," his wife whispered.

"Yes," smiled Orion, "everything ok?"

Sabina smiled in return and handed their son over to his father.

"Just fine," she said, "but I'd like a nap."

"Yes, yes, go. I'll take care of things for a spell."

She rose from the armchair and gave her back a stretch, "I reckon my arm would go dead if I'd sat there any longer."

"You're beautiful," replied Orion.

Sabina laughed; her husband could be impossibly maudlin. The baby boy was still awake and had not seemed to mind the change of hands supporting him. He cooed comfortably in his father's arms, and Orion could do little else but stare right back at the boy in marvel.

"I think he'd be smiling about now," said Sabina, "if he knew how to, that is."

It gets better. Orion realised then that life didn't need to get better, it was already pretty spectacular.

Sticks & Stones

"McKennark's a tosser!"

Young Treen, all sweat and energy, made a pretend pole-vault across Mr. McKennark's front gate and banged her stick on his window sill.

"Tosser! Tosser! Tosser!"

"Treen!" her mother called from across the boardwalk.

Doug and Kitty were in stitches laughing; Doug cackling so hard he rocked backwards on his perch and almost dragged his sister down with him as he tumbled.

"I said Treen!" cried Elanor, "Where did you learn that word?"

Treen skipped back to the veranda of her own home to where her mother sat in frustration. She brushed the leaves from her grubby shirt and pressed her hands to her hips, "Heard Uncle Vitus say it."

"Uncle Vitus is here?" came a weak voice, "or was it Titus? I had a son named Titus."

"No mum, Vitus is – oh for goodness' sake, Treen. You've got to stop pestering him. He's an old man, and I'm sure he doesn't appreciate you trespassing."

But the ribald girl wasn't listening; Treen had instead turned her attention to her brother and sister, who only egged her on with their uncontrolled laughter. Elanor's shoulders dropped, it was just all too hard. The times where she felt unheard were immeasurable, and often it was just better to relinquish any sense of control. Her mother sat next to her on the veranda, still as a statue, but with those rheumy eyes staring as though her own daughter was a stranger. Still though she was now, any movement made would set off a jitter that echoed her motions – a hand raised, followed by a shake, a turn of the head and it would bobble as though it could fall from her very shoulders.

"Mushrooms on sale," said the old lady, and Elanor wiped back a tear.

She'd be better off going the way of dad…

But then Elanor cursed herself for the thought. It was an evil thought, an easy way out. Her mother's madness had been a slow descent, like rust in an old engine, until the woman who'd once swept a younger Elanor off her feet when she was tired of walking was instead too feeble to hold a tea cup without dropping it. A fate worse than death – or was it? It wasn't as though Elanor's mother was aware of anything else. The woman just floated in a haze where neither past nor present held consequence. No, the terrible fate was held for those who came to her aid – or rather, for Elanor alone. Her father had left the picture long ago, pulling up stumps and heading the mines at Cardinal Mons. Cruel joke, Elanor had thought - that her old man would rather dig in the dirt than live any longer with her mother. Mind, this had been well before her mother's aging illness, a time where an outspoken wife was something that somehow shamed a man.

His loss. And it doesn't matter no more now he's gone.

But just as her father had held aloft some archaic banner of chauvinism, so too had her brother Vitus decided that it would be he who would represent the family at his funeral in the capital city.

"You've got the kids, El," he'd said, "and you're so good with mum."

And what about you then? A shackle on each limb, one child, two and three. And mum makes the quartet. No, big Vitus is too important for that – places to go, things to do. This swamp town of Banksia would sink into the shallows without such valour – Ha!

How was it that her drastically larger responsibilities somehow left her seen as too simple, too sheltered in her brother's mind? When he'd done nothing with his life, always bemoaning that the good times hadn't fallen into his lap, Elanor had gone and done what she had thought was her lot in rearing a bunch of children. Hindsight was a punishment; Elanor loved her children dearly but only realised too late that she could have done more for herself.

"Treen please. I won't ask again."

Her eldest daughter, the troublesome one, looking at her mother with contempt – Elanor chastised her free-spirit for the very qualities she wished she herself had seized. Treen at least dropped the stick she was carrying – an inch of rope given back to her struggling mum.

The girl's got heart, I just wish I didn't have to get this upset before she'd listen...

"But he yelled at Kit," said Treen.

"Well, that might be because she kept knocking on his front door and running. Come now, Treen, you know Mr. McKennark can't get up very well."

"M-money," chirped the old lady, "the baby is coming here?"

There was always a twinge of guilt accompanying the ways in which Elanor responded to her mother's ramblings; whether she'd try to explain a situation to her that she was not going to suddenly understand, the alternative being to simply ignore whatever she said. But the worst reaction of all was when Elanor simply agreed with whatever her mother had said. Sometimes it was just easier to do that than to correct her. And each time she did as such, Elanor hated herself all the more.

****

The tide was beginning to come in, and soon the mangrove roots would disappear under the shallows. Doug, who was Elanor's youngest, was picking his way through the mud beneath the boardwalks, carefully avoiding the roots like his life depended on it. To him, he was a ninja, expertly gliding betwixt the caltrops scattered by his adversaries. The aqua glow given off by the weedy sea dragons was becoming noticeable in the fading light of the day, and the beauty of dusk in Banksia leaked into the mangrove town. It was of utmost importance that Doug avoided treading on the mangrove roots - uncle Vitus had said so, and uncle Vitus was his best friend. He had told the young boy that the roots were what kept the whole tree together, and when the entire town was built upon a foundation of mangrove branches, well, Doug didn't need to be told twice just how vital those roots were. Still, he was a daring child, and in his attempts to impress his older sister Treen, he would try to catch the hermit crabs that scurried about the rising tide, carefully plucking them up by the shell while their little pincers flailed in retaliation.

"This one," he gasped, holding the creature by its spiral shell like a miniature ice cream cone. This crab was missing one pincer, and Doug suddenly felt sorry for the thing. Would Treen bat an eye to this? He'd captured a crippled crustacean while he'd known his sister to reel in enormous sea dragons that required two hands to carry.

"No," he concluded, and threw the crab back into the shallows; Treen was Doug's best friend - she deserved a more beautiful catch. You had to give girls beautiful things - that's what Doug had come to hold as his mantra. He liked it better when his mother laughed, something that had always been a rare occurrence. But at least she didn't cry as much anymore, not since his dad left, and Doug hated seeing his best friend cry.

Dad had made mum cry, this he knew, and Doug tried to make sure it wasn't his fault. He hadn't meant to tell his mother, tell her that his dad had hit him but it was only an accident. Doug had thought the woman in the chair was his grandmother, who'd forget what he said anyway, but no, it was mum, and she and dad had their biggest fight that evening. As he hid beneath the boardwalks with his sister Kitty he felt a strange relief; at least he'd only mentioned that one indiscretion. Truth was his father beat him all the time, and given the bruises he'd spied on his mum's arms at various times, he wasn't the only victim. Doug didn't like being hurt, but dad was his best friend - surely he didn't mean it.

And that's why dad left - he didn't want to hurt us anymore.

"Doug," cried Eleanor.

The boy withdrew from his reverie and noticed the water was up to his waist.

"Up here now, please. It's getting late,"

"Coming mum,"

****

The glow from the swamp gave an eerie inversion to the Banksia evening, as shadows were thrown upwards into the canopy of leaves and danced their way discreetly into the night sky above. It was difficult to tell where some of the shadows came from, as the ever-moving water warped the shapes of that which floated in it and haunted the more fanciful imaginations of those who observed it. Candles weren't used in the town, given the risk of fire, and the authorities that presided over Banksia had yet to find an engineer with the smarts to run electricity to the homesteads. As such the swamp lights were often the only source of luminance for the residents until the sun made its return in the east. Meals were cooked on heavily guarded flames, in little ovens comprised of stones collected from inland, and the mild weather meant that the nights were warm enough to sleep comfortably with little more than a blanket or two.

Kitty lay wedged between her older sister and younger brother under a clammy leather blanket. Sleeping in the middle was frustrating, especially when she needed to use the toilet in the middle of the night, or worse still when she had to move over to allow Doug the same requirement. The young girl yearned for her own bedroom; a place she might have just for herself, where she might embellish the walls with decorations of an identity - that when others saw the room they'd say 'yes, surely this is Kitty's room,'

Sadly, her features were boring, her personality plain, and Kitty often found herself pinballing through her youth trying to establish just what kind of person she was meant to be. Being the middle child meant she did not carry the task of leadership and responsibility expected of Treen, nor was she afforded the forbearant clemency extended to her little brother. Funny to consider she was such an outsider whilst standing, metaphorically, in the middle of the family combine. Lacking the exuberance of Treen and the innocence of Doug, Kitty would search for any scrap of knowledge that she might impart on those who'd listen. Surely to be interesting, she must know of interesting things, and she loved to be the one who said 'I told you so,'

"There've been *heaps* of UFO sightings lately," she mumbled to her siblings.

"Says who?" Treen snorted.

"Says me! Saw the newspaper up-branch at the store. Bunch of weird people appearing in strange places."

"How can they be UFOs if they don't fly?"

Kitty felt a hot rush of frustration; her sister was always trying to undermine her, "Aliens I meant. They look like us but talk funny. That's how you know it's them."

"You're so full of shit, Kitty,"

Doug gasped, "Treen, you can't say that!"

"I am not!" said Kitty, "Lukey agreed with me, he read most of the bigger words for me,"

"Lukey? That weirdo at the store? Well now I know it's bullshit," said Treen.

Poor Doug continued to object, "I'm gonna tell mum if you keep talking bad like that,"

"Shush, Doug!" Treen could sense Kitty seething in the darkness of the bedroom - her little sister was so dumb sometimes, "you're gullible, Kit; is that a big word you can understand? Full of shit - shitty Kitty, haha!"

"More like *you* shush…" mumbled Doug.

Kitty's fury subsided as quickly as it had arisen, "Leave me alone…"

"All I'm saying is don't believe everything you read, especially when it's that idiot Lukey telling you - that guy will latch onto any wild conspiracy,"

"I believe you, Kitty," whispered Doug, even though he was not so sure.

But Kitty had decided she would talk no longer that night; there was no reasoning with her big sister. She felt doomed to play second fiddle for the rest of her life.

****

The night was still; not a breath of wind shifted the mangrove leaves as Eleanor lay awake in the other bedroom.

They should be sleeping… she thought, *but God I love to hear them prattle.*

Across the room her mother snored softly, another difficult day where she had survived. Eleanor wondered if the old lady's dreams were as muddled as her waking thoughts. Was the embrace of sleep an escape from the hazy world she no longer knew?

Eleanor sincerely hoped that God was not so cruel, yet maybe it made no difference either way. Her mother would die soon, just as her father had, and the demented woman wouldn't even realise it was happening. Where had her mother gone? Was she as good as dead already? All that remained was a husk of a human, still performing its vital functions, but those traits that made life so wonderful - memories, experience, love - they had long disintegrated. Eleanor's mother was still there, but at the same time she was not - she had no other way of explaining it.

It would be better for her to think of other matters. Eleanor knew what Kitty had been talking of - strange people appearing in unusual places; she knew because Vitus had sent a letter explaining the delay of his return to town. The train he had been on had hit one of them. The accident had happened up in the mountains of all places, and her brother had been shuttled back to Cardinal Mons for an extra night layover.

Thank God I didn't end up going to dad's funeral then.... Eleanor thought with little remorse, *stuck in another town with my darling little screamers? Hard pass.*

Her kids had provided a feasible excuse for her to avoid the funeral; they were just too rambunctious, and trying to wrangle them through a big city like that was asking for trouble. Her father had been glib in his abandonment, and frankly Eleanor was happy to return the favour in one final insult. He might have abandoned his children, but she would do what was best for her own. In all honesty she had not thought of her father in years, and met news of his death with little more than a shrug; the distant sadness lingered as it always had, but she was surprised that it showed no added barbs in wake of the death. First her dad, then that fool she had married, had given Eleanor no reason to continue trusting the male sex; even her brother Vitus betrayed glimpses of that congenital arrogance she now so despised and perhaps unfairly painted all men with.

Eleanor was getting too worked up to sleep. The tide of rest, and the rejuvenation it should bring, always washed in with the polluted waters of life's troubles rather than its soothing embrace of indifference. The train that Vitus had been on had hit a man - a tragic event, but it was due to a more sinister reason that the story had made the papers. Eleanor recalled the letter from her brother, *some clown hit on the tracks - will be late back. A few days maybe,* and then the bizarre article about the event. It was indisputable fact that a man had been struck, dragged some fifteen metres beneath the cold and massive weight of the locomotive; knowable even in the mangled state in which the corpse was discovered. But it had been the colour of the blood - a deep crimson with black hues, almost purple in colour - that had baffled the coroner and captured the morbid imagination of the common folk reading the papers. It had originally been written off as mere coal dust mixed with blood, until another sample taken from one of the more *intact* portions of the poor dead man confirmed the anomaly. It was blood alright, or whatever this man, this *thing*, used as blood, but its properties were not like any similar substance known by medical science. Whether the man had some unknown illness or had perhaps succumbed to some kind of poisonous reaction was inconclusive. The location of the incident also had the authorities scratching their heads - why the man had been in such a remote area of the countryside was anyone's guess.

Eleanor rolled over and pulled the blanket over her eyes.

Sleep now. Stop thinking.

Her body began to drift into a blissful slumber but it was jerked awake by the sound of Kitty screaming. Eleanor shot up instantly and heard Treen speak next, "Eww! Doug wet the bed again!"

The exhausted mother resided in the fact that she would not get much sleep that night.

Creaking of the Beam

The hour in which Cardinal Mons threw its shadow over Peatstack had drifted by mechanically, and the mid-morning sun was beginning to shine through the smog of the smokestacks. Sunlight curled around the mountain summit in serpentine rays, and were the Peatstack residents able to see its shimmers reflected off the snow caps, they'd no doubt stand in awe of nature's beauty. But such had been the modern age in this mining town, that the gold fields of wheat had been forced to share a similar pallet with a sky polluted by refinery smoke. The smokestacks belched their ochre fumes from above the sawtooth roofs of factories, and though the locomotives were nourished by the massive coal loaders pouring that precious fuel into their tenders, the nearby crops ached with the inhalations of waste poisoning the old irrigation channels. The town stood as one of the worst mistakes made in the history of The Continent; a land so rich in diverse nature, with a government that had long embraced clean energy and a symbiotic relationship with the land that fed them. But the people of Verdigris needed fuel for their trains, and the opulent folk in Magna Austinus were hardly going to give up their wealth of gemstones any time soon. No - the capital city of The Continent was happy enough to draw attention to itself and distract the observer's eye from the dingy settlement at the mountain's base like a dirty secret that must remain hidden. If anything, most folk (even those who called Peatstack home) were relieved to be hidden in shadows for half the average day, as the sun slid across the sky. Frankly, if Magna Austrinus was seen as the immaculate face of The Continent, then Peatstack could be considered, well, a more unsavoury part of the anatomy. Not that its humble dwellers were devoid of patriotism, quite the contrary. There were many miners who would argue that without them, the rest of society would suffer, for Peatstack contributed so much to the economy and lifestyle of the entire land. Could they bear the cross of toil and squalor for the sake of the rest? Those who toil were lifted, apparently, but Peatstack was still awaiting its turn.

The streets were still dirty tracks with little in way of guttering, meaning stormwater would not wash them clean but rather coagulate into uneven puddles of filth; a man would do well to avoid wearing his dress shoes in such a place. And unfortunately, the deciduous trees lining the sidewalks spent three quarters of the year bare of leaves, adding more shades of brown to this sepia town. The kids in the street were bored; their oft-absent parents were honest toilers doing what they could to make a living, and as such the local police had had to implement a daily scour of the streets to round up truant children who tried to skip school.

On the main boulevard of Peatstack stood the local courthouse - one of the nicer buildings in town - and it was here that Officer Ernie Burstwhile returned after his morning corralling of naughty school kids. It was the worst part of his job; the kids showed no hesitation in taunting the poor cop, poking fun at his weight and resolutely ignoring his orders for them to move along. And he was never one for disciplining, even as a cop; most of the time he'd be assigned simpler jobs such as writing tickets. Even his own children had taken advantage of his timid nature, for a time at least, they'd softened towards their old man after their mother had died when they were young. Ernie Burstwhile was a man plagued by the past, by a life he no longer had, and the one partner he'd had to help him navigate cruelty of the world ripped away from him too soon. She'd been gone close to fifteen years, taken in a way that Ernie still refused to speak about, yet still her influence clung to him like barnacles to a hull and, much as an old ship can no longer voyage with a rust-struck body without fear of sinking, Ernie never strayed too far from what he deemed safe. It saddened the locals to see, for he was at least well-liked for his police work, and he knew that many treated him with a gentle sympathy that was, to him, rather petty, for not many would have understood what he'd experienced.

One such local was Tabby Garth, a fellow cop whose careful kindness towards Ernie had drifted into frustrated indifference. She watched Ernie hoist himself from his vehicle and lock the door, only to turn back and double check the car was, in fact, locked.

See? That's the kind of shit that really bugs me, Tabby mused to nobody but herself, *we get it, life's been rough, but must you be such a downer?*

But she then pictured the unattractive man sitting alone in his kitchen parlour and suddenly hated herself for beating down on someone so pathetic, even if it was unspoken.

"Howdy Ern,"

"Tab. Morning,"

"Yer coffee's probably right cold by now, sorry,"

"Damn kids held me up," replied Ernie. He sipped from the paper cup handed to him and winced at its tepid flavour, "still wakes me up at least."

"Keep telling you I can do the kid scour if you want," said Tabby.

"Naw, 'ppreciate it but I like to stretch the legs to start the day. Almost makes the verbal abuse from those little shits worth it."

"Hear."

Together they made a rather comically heavyset duo; him with slouched shoulders loaded with the weight of a middle-aged paunch, and her needing to wrap her belt beneath her ribs - the smallest circumference her plump torso could offer. The long arm of the law stretched across Peatstack only, and often wheezed with the exertion of one woefully out of shape. Small town meant small crimes though, and it wasn't likely that the law enforcement of Peatstack would need to develop a sharp fitness any time soon.

They entered the courthouse, a smell of old leather and linoleum stung the nostrils of those new to the building, but for these two cops it was simply a part of the job. Policing wasn't a picnic, and why should it smell like one? Their shoes squeaked down the cold corridor past the offices, where crestfallen workers could be seen betwixt the Venetian blinds going about their mundane duties.

"Boss brief you?" asked Tabby Garth.

Ernie Burstwhile shook his head.

"Well this will be fun for you then."

They entered a small windowless room used for interviews, where there sat a peculiar man at the table in the centre. Ernie never spoke first in these situations, just in case he was too friendly with someone who wound up being pretty rotten.

Tabby was always better at the interrogation stuff anyhow... Wonder what this scum bag is in for?

Tabby Garth handed him a clipboard detailing the subject in front of them and began to speak plainly to the man while Ernie read.

"So, our strange little squatter. Sleep ok last night?"

The man, who Ernie now realised was handcuffed to the table, lifted his shaggy head and smirked at Tabby.

"Right good. 'bout as comfortable as the factory floor."

His breath was horrible, Ernie could smell it from across the room as poignant scribbles stood out from the clipboard paper - like 'trespass', 'uncooperative' and other five-dollar words. The stranger slouched in his chair like a pile of clothes, the billowing coat draped over him disguising any sort of shape or figure.

He seemed malnourished however, that much was discernible, and filthy to boot.

Tabby continued, "Aye, reckon a fella must have some place nicer to call home? Some place that belongs to 'im?"

"Well, the fields were too cold," said the stranger, "so I found a place with a roof."

"Funny guy, hey?" said Ernie.

Tabby shook her head, "Now I asked you to fill out your details for me and you haven't. Do I assume you can't read? Or are you merely defiant?"

"Don't know what that is," said the stranger.

"Details," said Tabby, "let's start with your name. Whadda we call you?"

"I suppose you can call me... Daddy Long-Legs,"

The two cops gazed at each other, bemused.

"You suppose?" said Ernie.

"Yanking my chain, boyo," said Tabby, "but I'll play. Who can verify that you're Daddy Long-Legs? Family? Friends? Where's your place of residence?"

"In the factory. Well, not anymore I guess,"

Tabby sighed, "Look friend. Trying to be nice here, but you're making it hard. Now old Halroy says he found you in his paper factory - realise that's trespassing? That it's dangerous to be around all those machines?"

"I only wanted to sleep," said Daddy Long-Legs, "didn't touch anything,"

"Missing the point, guy," said Tabby, "now I can see you've had a rough go at it. Can't give me a proper name, no place of residence, no kin to explain your appearance in this here town. I see you need some help; I want to get you a spot down the shelter, really, I do. But if you can't co-operate with me, I'm going to have to stick you back in the cells, understand?"

"That's ok with me."

The man who called himself Daddy Long-Legs remained handcuffed in place as the two cops stepped outside.

"A character," said Ernie.

"Fuckin' dust-heads, I tell you," Tabby swore, "he ain't the only one neither - sarge over at Jindee station told me about some bloke assaulted by a weird character in a cabin up the slopes. Reckons the weirdo was right nuts, couldn't speak properly, answer questions or anything. Sounds similar to our man in there."

"Maybe it is?" suggested Ernie.

Tabby shook her head, "Nah I only mention it as coincidence - timeline don't match up. Plus, the assault charge led to an arrest at the lodge in question earlier this morning,"

"Weird shit, I agree," said Ernie, "plus that strange body found on the tracks round the mountain side - I read it didn't seem quite human, but certainly weren't no animal either,"

"Ha, come now Burstwhile. You ain't suggesting we got a little alien monster sitting in that meeting room, do ya?"

"No, I guess not,"

"It's gotta be drugs. The time of year. Lonely folk get bored and desperate for attention - even to the point of getting arrested,"

"I'll have to try it someday,"

"Ha! Ass..."

"So, what do we do with him then?"

Tabby shrugged, "Well I got nothing. Guy hasn't shared a scrap of anything worth a buck. He'll be in the cells again tonight most like, though you know as well as I that's a temporary fix."

"Get the feel he'd stay there forever if he could,"

"I hear. Exactly. If he's without a home of his own then a roof would be a haven, be it a cell or no. Aww who knows, Ern. I'll try and get him a spot at the shelter, get him rehabilitated. But he don't seem the sort to even know how to work or anything,"

Ernie was attempting to pour himself a cup of water from the cooler but only succeeded in splashing the stuff all over his pants; Tabby winced and sucked her teeth.

"Look Ern; plans tonight?"

"What do you think?"

"I know, I know. Look, I'm always going to offer. Don't want to come across as inclusive - that goes for all of us. Seriously though, pub after hours. We're there every night. Would be great if you joined us, I reckon you need it,"

"I'll think about it,"

"Sure you will,"

Ernie sighed, "One day I will, Tab. Don't give up on me."

"Hold ya to it."

He drove home that evening pleased that he had spoken with people that day. Since the kids had grown up and moved out there were often quieter days where the sun would set without him having said a word.

Those days made him the saddest - but today had been a good day - good in a painfully average way. Sometimes he spoke to the car radio, silly as that may have been, but today he was happy just to listen.

"... Man found brutally mangled in an elevator car in..."

"Christ..." He muttered, "always someone having a worse day than ya,"

Dad always said that, he thought, *wonder if that's ever false? Wonder if you could have a worse day than literally everyone? 'spose someone has to have it the worst...*

The meat he'd left on the kitchen sink had defrosted. Food again. What was the point? Ernie cooked, and ate, barely tasting, and washed up with such mechanical precision that he was amazed how late it had become when he finally checked the time. He sat down at the kitchen table and grasped the telephone receiver in his meaty hand, dialling one of the two phone numbers he memorised. It rang once before he slammed the receiver down.

No, not him. Poor boy holds onto things too much.

Ernie rang the second number, and three rings later a voice answered.

His own voice faltered, his heart raced on a sudden, "Hey sweetie,"

"Dad," came the reply, "it's good to hear your voice,"

"You too, Trid,"

There was an awkward pause, but Ernie's daughter kept her warm tone, "Is everything alright?"

"Was gunna call your brother," he stammered, "but you know what he's like with talkin' and all,"

Astrid laughed, "Like you, dad?"

"Heh. Yeah, yeah you got me there,"

His scalp was glossed with sweat beneath the dim kitchen light, and there was another pause.

"Listen, I was just thinking what your mother would say if she could see you. And Manny. You know, see the woman, erm, man - adults. Adults that you grew up to be," his voice was choked.

"I miss her too, dad. Hard day, was it?"

"No. No actually. And that's just the thing. She was just, I don't know. At the forefront of my mind today. You know?"

"Of course,"

"I often wonder if - uh,"

He lost his voice.

"If you could've changed it?"

He couldn't respond.

"Dad. Mum was unwell. Wasn't thinking straight. It played out how it played out. Nothing changes that."

"I know you're right. I think. I hope. I just needed to, you know,"

"It's ok dad. You're allowed to feel that way," Astrid paused before continuing, "but you're allowed to live now too, you know."

"Yep. Yep, yeah totally. You always had that about you. Knowing what to say, that is."

"Learnt from her."

"I know."

There was a short silence.

"Listen dad, come holidays I'll be coming by old Peatstack. I'll make sure of it. I wish it could be sooner but -"

"No I understand completely. It's not that, it's just. Needed to hear your voice,"

"I love you dad."

"Love you too, girl."

"I - huh? Look I gotta go, Trish has just knocked her bowl off the table," her voice began to rush, "she's walking now - clumsy as hell but pretty cute. I can't wait for you to see."

Ernie smiled, "Give her a kiss from poppy."

"I will dad. Talk soon."

He hung up the phone and sank into the midweek silence, suddenly aware of the refrigerator motor humming softly, and the buzz of the fluorescent light above him. He thought he felt a chill in the air, but that might have just been the slow pulse of his blood as he sat paralysed in the deafening quiet. Finding some reserve of energy, Ernie rose to his feet, legs first before his shoulders and head rolled out like a sunflower; every action he made felt deliberate and thought-out, as if forgetting the mechanics of breathing would cause his lungs to stop. The kitchen window was pitch black - if he hadn't known the yard beyond, it could have been an outlook on the edge of existence. Ernie poured a glass of water and stared into that dark space, a moonless night, and visualised the outline of the things he knew to be there - his row of rose bushes, the potting shed, the shovel and wheelbarrow awaiting their next task. And as the wind blew down from Cardinal Mons, the yard came to life in the tenebrous tide with the hush of leaves and the creak of trees. The creaking - God how he hated the sound; the hanging ferns creaking in their pots in the shed, those little chains wrapped about the paint chipped beams. *And who knew a wooden beam could be used for that?* The thought had never crossed his mind until she - yes, the creaking. He hated the sound so much. He couldn't think about that anymore tonight. Ernie decided instead to think about the strange man he'd met today, Daddy Long-Legs, and whether he had somewhere to sleep, out of the wind, away from those teasing tendrils. He thought of the track his life had followed that ended with him meeting such a peculiar man, and whether he'd remember this day in another fifteen years, or if it would be forgotten, carried off by the mountain wind betwixt the potted ferns and into the wheat fields beyond the town.

Afterforward

The stars dotted helpless in darkness, branching aimlessly into oblivion, little blossoms calling to one another through the gloom. Yet the calls would go unanswered, fallen upon the deaf black of space. And maybe some of these stars had gathered pebbles from the astral tide, and spun them about their centre like a mobile; planets too small to even discern with the eye, dwarfed by the enormity of their parent star, which itself was but a pinprick on the night sky. And maybe each pinprick could link to another, and then another, and another ad infinitum, until none stood out from the gabardine stitching of woven quasars. All of this space junk – and what purpose did it serve other than to be known? Was the immensity of the universe proof of a God's inconceivable love, or of a catastrophic indifference? Past the ice planets and the gas giants, to the Rings of Mars and the Major and Minor Moons – opalescent and cardinal – inward to that one lonely planet. And there, floating on a Southern Ocean, Verdigris – alone, so alone.

The abrupt ending and number within the title should affirm that this book is indeed one part of a greater story. Whilst the ending has been planned, it remains unwritten, and until as such I would implore you, reader, to theorise what might have happened to the people of Verdigris.

What befell Balfour? Did Lucida fulfil her adventurous yearning? Who of Libra and Spindle would emerge victorious? And what of those mysterious characters inflicted by a more mysterious illness?

When we read stories, we indelibly become a part of them for however long they last; when we at last set aside that book, we know no more of its characters – only that which the author divulged. Yet their lives would no doubt continue, as does your own, and in that sense anything remains possible. Until this story is completed, you are free to create any future you wish for the people of Verdigris, and perhaps they, within closed pages, will propound their own theories about you.

- P.S.C.

About the author:

P.S.Clinen lives in New South Wales, Australia. He has written several novels and works of poetry and releases music under the name Pinnacle Tricks. All of his works can be found online.

Made in United States
Orlando, FL
20 June 2024